Prai

D0555721

"Meliza Bañales' stories of growing up Chicana in LA break you open then stab you in your flaming heart with a switchblade. The only girl whose lines make me cry. Every time."

—Lynn Breedlove, lead singer of Tribe 8 and
Winner of a 2010 Lambda Literary Award

"…she fire(s) out all the dirty details with impassioned rhythmic intensity while keeping the mood light."

—*The Boston Phoenix*

"Meliza Bañales is one of the best writers I know— period. Her writing on queer punk mixed Chicana femme 90s survivor life tells totally real stories with beauty that will burn you clean, open your eyes and tell it exactly how it is."

—Leah Lakshmi Piepzna-Samarashinha,
Lambda Award winning author of
Love Cake and *Bodymap*

L a d y b o x .

♥

A Ladybox Original

Ladybox Books
10765 SW Murdock Lane
Apt. G6
Tigard, OR 97224

Copyright © 2015 by Meliza Bañales

Cover art and design copyright © 2015 by Matthew Revert
www.matthewrevert.com

Interior design by J David Osborne

ISBN: 978-1-940885-29-2

Printed in the USA.

LIFE IS WONDERFUL, PEOPLE ARE TERRIFIC

by
Meliza Bañales

LADYBOX BOOKS
PORTLAND, OR

TABLE OF CONTENTS

For us—the freaks, weirdos, punks, feministas, radicals, poc's, mixed-race folks, queers, dykes, homos, poor kids, hustlers, orphans, hermosas, working girls, ladies on poles, dreamers

POTENTIAL

There's something about waking-up with a hang-over that reminds you, 'Yes, you have a body. And a mind. And now you have to deal with it.'

The sun was sharp. Clear. I've lived near oceans my whole life and at the sake of sounding really fucking shallow, I only chose this school because it was near the ocean and had a well-known punk-scene. And it's an hour away from San Francisco. But three weeks in and I'm already well on my way to self-sabotage. As proven by my current meeting with the Dean of Student Affairs.

"You know Missy—you can call me Ruth—we are on the quarter system and so if anyone is already falling behind in the first three weeks it doesn't look good…"

"Okay."

"You are here on a scholarship…"

"Okay."

"I know that Brown University offered you a place. It's clear you're very bright. But, here in Santa Cruz we aren't just concerned with brightness."

"Okay."

"We're concerned with a total, well-rounded individual. You know? A spiritual, grounded, eager warrior of knowledge who wants to explore the depths of their own consciousness…"

Under my dark glasses I could see the outline of the redwoods through her office window. In Los Angeles there are trees but no forest. I'm going to a school in the forest and it's clear that I didn't think this shit all the way through.

"As you know Missy, we don't have 'grades'—those arbitrary letters that are supposed to determine a person's intelligence and skill. No. Here in Santa Cruz we have evaluations so we can really show how you shine or where you need to pick up the torch a little bit…"

My head was fucking killing me. Once again, this was my fault. I'm always drinking in the wrong order: beer before liquor.

"There's only six weeks left until finals and then poof—the quarter is over, the courses are finished, and you move forward. So you see why I have to have this talk with you now."

The bean bag I was in felt like a comfortable stomach, only not at work. And she sat on one of those yoga balls, gently bouncing up and down. The forest was still there and so was the vodka in my backpack.

"I feel like you're really receiving me right now, Missy. I can tell that you're a deep person and you're really feeling the positive energy that I'm sending out to you right now, right now in this moment. So can

I count on you to be more energetically open to this place, to this new plane?"

"Okay."

"Is it really okay? You know, I'm your friend here. Go ahead—tell me what you're thinking."

"Well, I'm drunk."

"Yes, yes—drunk. We're all drunk in one way or the other, you're so right."

"No, I'm drunk."

"I know, I know. It's so easy to get drunk in this place," Ruth chimed.

"You're tellin' me."

"It's so easy to get drunk in the trees and smelling the ocean. In all the wide, open space that The Universe offers each of us in our lives."

"Right…"

"Yeah, do you mind if I just get down to your level?" Ruth said smiling. She hopped off the ball and got into a bean bag beside me.

"Tell me more about being drunk? I'm really liking this connection we're making, Missy."

"Look, I'm really drunk—"I said.

"Yes, yes keep saying it—the more we say it the more we feel it, believe it, be it. Be drunk."

She closed her eyes and took deep breaths.

"Seriously, 'Ruth', I'm drunk," I said, sitting up and opening my back pack.

I pulled out the bottle of vodka from my bag and showed it to her. She looked at the bottle. Then me. Then the bottle.

"Oh, I see, I see…" Her smile faded.

"So if there isn't anything else?" I said.

She tried to smile at me as I got up, took my bag and the bottle and walked out the door and down the wooded path. It was about 8:30 in the morning, Monday. I hadn't been back to my tiny room in the woods for three days. I just took the bus back from my other house with JB in San Francisco. Working weekends in the city was okay except when you were a stripper, which I was. It was long nights and I couldn't drink and I got bored easily. But three hundred and fifty dollars later I reminded myself that it wasn't so bad. Plus JB was almost never there because he was touring with his band most of the time and being a big-bad-punk-rock-piece-of-shit-legend. It was cool.

I finally reached my door and it hit me that I was pretty alone. For the first time in my life. I was eighteen and alone. There was a letter on my desk from my brother. I always knew it was from him because it had been opened, then resealed with a sticker on it that said "LA County Jail."

Guerita,

You're a big college girl now. I'm still here waiting for my court date. Thanks for coming to see me before you made your big exit. Things don't look so good for me. My lawyer thinks I might be here awhile and then there's whatever happens next. Just keep ya head up, flaca. And don't let know one tell you nothing. Remember where you're from.

I took out a pen and corrected the 'know' in "no one". It was the student in me. I wasn't a complete fuck-up. There were just times I was really good at not caring.

I knew I had shit to do but I couldn't remember any of it. I just laid down and let the day figure itself out.

NEO-NAZIS FUCKING SUCK

I was leaving another class, walking alone in the forest. Three weeks and already I was sitting in the Dean's office. And still no friends in Santa Cruz. But I had JB.

JB, or Jackoff Bluegrass, was a living punk legend, the front-man and lyricist for one of the best bands ever and a huge reason I wanted to get to San Francisco. His band, Sour Grapes, was the real birth of hardcore on the west coast in the 80's, when he was just twenty-one. I was fourteen when I saw them play in LA and it was like God was not only really up there, but smiling on me. Punk rock changed my life at the age of thirteen and I was hell-bent on being a good fan. I started sending letters and postcards to the address on the back of one of his records. I didn't really expect him to write back. But it became a weird monthly tradition of mine to at least send something. When I was almost eighteen, a postcard came to my parents' tiny house in our neighborhood and it read:

Hey Missy,

Thanks for all the years of loyalty. If you're ever in San Francisco and need a hand, gimme a call.
—JB

A phone number was written below his name. I wanted to call it right away out of excitement but I decided that I wouldn't. I was gonna save it for when I did need it. It was then that there was no doubt in my mind that I had to make it to San Francisco some way, no matter what.

I'd only been at the college two weeks when I decided to take the last Greyhound bus of the day from Santa Cruz to the city. A girl I danced with in LA moved up there and gotten a job at a club in North Beach. She knew I needed work and invited me up for an audition. When I got to the station, I pulled out the postcard, dropped twenty cents into the payphone and tried the number JB gave me. It rang about four times and just as I was about to hang-up in defeat, the call was answered and a voice came over the phone.

"What."

"Um, it's me, Missy."

Fuck—I already sounded fuckin' stupid. 'It's me, Missy.' Like he really knew me. I was a dumbass.

There was a pause on the phone.

"Is this the Missy from LA whose been writing me since 1992? Cuz honestly that's the only Missy that comes to mind..." the voice said.

"Yes!" I shouted, overly excited. "I mean, yes, yes it is."

"Are you in San Francisco?"

"Yeah—actually I'm at the Greyhound station downtown."

"That's cool—if you have seventy-five cents, go to Mission Street and catch the 14 MUNI towards Balboa Park. Get off at 19th Street. Call me from the payphone on the corner and I'll come down. Otherwise, I'll see you around."

"No! No, I have seventy-five cents. I'm on my way."

"Cool."

Then he hung-up. I couldn't believe it—he knew who I was, really knew who I was. I raced out of the Greyhound station, caught the bus like he asked, made the call at the corner. There was no answer and I was out of change. After a few minutes the door to a tiny store-front opened and there he was, right there in the flesh.

"I was taking an epic piss so I couldn't get to the phone. But I figured it was you so I walked my ass down here to check. You hungry?"

We walked up a narrow staircase and went through another door and entered his apartment. It was a lot bigger than I expected and though most of the furniture was milk crates, cement blocks, and bean bags, it was pretty clean.

"Welcome to Chez Bluegrass," he said.

After chips and dip, endless stories from both sides, and about a six pack later JB popped the question.

"So, you wanna live here or something?"

"Well, I wasn't expecting—"

"Look I'm not hitting on you, you don't have to get weird. It's just you said you're gonna be working here so you may need a place to crash a few nights a week and it just so happens that my piece-of-shit housemate had to ditch-out on me at the last minute. I know this place isn't much, but it's clean and cheap and there's a tiny room right there that was supposed to be a closet that's big enough for a small bed and dresser if you want it. There's even a window in there."

"That's...awesome. But, I don't have much money right now..."

"How much you got?"

I pulled an envelope out of my pocket that had all the money I had in the world: Five hundred dollars..

"Well why don't you gimme two-hundred dollars and we'll say it's rent and deposit. You can just kick me down a hundred and fifty around the first of the month and we're cool."

"Seriously?"

"Sure, why not. You seem like you don't have your head up your ass."

And that was it—I was officially living in San Francisco, part-time, with one of the most famous punks alive. JB was my first friend in my new life, my welcoming committee I guess. It was fucking unbelievable.

After three weeks, I realized that my only friend was gone. A lot. And I was alone. A lot. I did get the job at the new club, Harry's. It was kind of like the fast-food of dancing but it paid and the club was all kinds of strict so I felt safe there. I was only in the city Friday through Sunday. Every time I would return to the school in the woods I felt so empty. The week was always so fucking long. And not to brag, but my classes were pretty easy which only gave me more time to either fuck off or just be fucking depressed over my lack of real human connection.

I decided to be brave: I was gonna go to shows in Santa Cruz. Alone. I was a girl so I had no idea what I would really be walking into. I walked around downtown looking for flyers. After a half hour I found one for a show at the Vets Hall. It was in Spanish and English which relieved me a little because most of the punks that I was friends with in LA were Mexican, like me. The show was five dollars for four bands. I figured I had to start somewhere.

I came to discover that almost all the punk shows in Santa Cruz happened at the Vets Hall, an actual U.S. Veterans Hall. The vets who ran it were so hard up for money that they finally gave-in to renting it to punk bands to cover expenses. There were countless bands in town and the original venue for shows was shut-down a few years earlier. No one would rent to them, for obvious reasons. Look, let's face it. Most of these bands were hardcore bands and lived with the drinking and drama that came with that. But it looked like everyone came to an agreement and all punk roads led to the Santa Cruz Vets Hall.

When I entered, the space was huge, like a hall where you would have a wedding reception or a quinceñera. There was a stage and a descent sound system. There was also a basement which was smaller but rented out for cheap if you couldn't afford the upstairs. That's where this first show was. I walked down, paid my money, and leaned against the wall in the farthest part of the room, tucked away. I was nervous. I wanted to meet people but I was also comfortable with being anonymous. It was kind of a fucked up situation, I think they call it a Catch-22. I read that book before but didn't really get it. The show started and everything seemed familiar, cool even. No stupid dudes tried to get into my pants and for the most part, the bands weren't that bad. The final band came on and it was a Mexican punk band named Los Illegales. They were fucking amazing. I felt like I could loosen up and I walked up a little closer. I also saw some other girls there which made me relax more. This exercise of going to a show by myself was turning out pretty fucking okay. When the show ended, everyone helped clean up and it made me feel like I was finally making myself at home.

I made it outside to catch the bus back to school when I saw a Chicana, maybe about fifteen-years-old, alone and looking a little worried. After about ten minutes of watching her from the corner of my eye, I realized she was crying. By this point the Vets Hall was dark, everyone was gone. There was just the two of us out there. I walked over to her.

"Hey, are you okay?"

She looked up at me from the curb, eyeliner smeared all over her face.

"I came here with my friends and they left me. I don't have any money and if I call my older cousin I stay with he's gonna fucking kill me. I don't know what to do," she sniffled.

"Well, where do you live?"

"Watsonville," she said.

I had no idea where the fuck that was. It was midnight and she really looked so fucking stressed. I looked around to make sure there was nobody hiding in the bushes. It could have been a set up to pounce on me and rob my ass. But the coast was clear, so I took a chance.

"Well, my name is Missy. I have enough to take the bus. If there's a bus that goes to where you live I'll ride with you and pay for it, make sure you get home. You can tell your cousin you were with me so you don't get in trouble."

"Really? That would be so fucking cool. My name is Angie. I think the last bus leaves the Metro station in fifteen minutes."

We walked to the Metro station where all the buses in town left. She wiped her face up with a napkin I gave her from my pocket. The bus ride was only thirty minutes and even though she was a few years younger than me, we couldn't stop talking and laughing. When her stop came, she thanked me and faded into the dark.

It turned out that Angie's older cousin, Juan, was the uncle of the lead singer of Los Illegales, Mario Rodriguez. A week later they all sought me out at another show to thank me for being so cool to her and just like that, I had some friends to kick it with.

I was going to at least four shows a week with my new friends, getting drunk on the beach, discovering Watsonville—a tiny, Mexican farm-working community about twenty miles from Santa Cruz—and feeling like my new life was a perfect fit. For the first time in my life, I was getting everything I wanted.

It was another Saturday afternoon in the Beach Flats with my new friends, Angie, Juan, Mario, and Mario's fourteen-year-old little brother, Hector. We were hanging out in the parking lot of this hotel where some of the day laborers around here stay at. It was always chill over there and reminded me of LA. Lots of Mexicans, the sunshine, the sound of Radio Romantica blaring through shitty speakers out of someone's window, and beer. We were an odd looking crew, being that I had a shaved head and combat boots all the time, Angie and Hector looked punk with an indie edge, Mario was straight-up punk, mohawk, vest and all. There was Juan, the oldest of our group at thirty-three dressed in classic vato style with creased Dickies, black and white Cortez's, plain white tee tucked in. I didn't care what people thought. We looked cool and acted cooler.

On this afternoon, I was already a six-pack in on my own. It was unusually warm that day and I just kept drinking beer after beer. Until the laughter stopped and it got real quiet.

"Take a look esé," Juan said to Mario.

There were two white guys coming towards us. Both had shaved heads, tattoos I couldn't decipher, white tees, jeans rolled up, and Doc Martin boots with white and red laces. It didn't set-off any alarms for me so I kept drinking and hanging-out. But everyone else was tense.

"Look, you know I just took care of my warrant. I can't get hot up in here, Mario," Juan said.

"Let's just leave right now," Angie insisted.

Everyone was in on something I clearly wasn't.

"Just be cool everybody. If anything happens, I need you to take the girls and my brother," Mario said to Juan.

"I'm not sayin' I'm just gonna leave you here, holmes," Juan replied.

"Just do it homie—you know how it goes and they need you to look out for them. I'll be okay."

The two white guys were still staring right at us, coming up on us faster. When they got close enough, I could make out one of the tattoos on one of the guy's right arm: it was a portrait of Adolf Hilter. It was then that in my half-drunken state all the pieces were coming together. They were neo-Nazis and those guys were always trouble no matter how you sliced it. I tried to be cool like my friends but I could feel my heart about to burst out of my fucking chest. They were coming closer and closer until finally they were maybe twenty feet away from us. At that moment, one of the guys pulled something out of his back. It was a big ass gate chain. The other guy pulled out a crow-bar, and then out of nowhere three more white dudes with shaved heads and the whole fascist uniform came out on the sides from nowhere.

"Fucking run. Now," Mario said under his breath.

I dropped my beer and Angie, Hector, and me started running.

"Get those fuckin' spics that just took off!" one of the Nazis yelled to another.

I turned my head to see if Juan was behind us, but he was with Mario and the two of them were fighting off three Nazis with chains, crow-bars, and bats. I turned back around and kept fucking running. There were two Nazis chasing us and they were fucking fast motherfuckers.

"We're gonna get you fucking wetbacks! You can't run forever you stupid spics!" the Nazis yelled.

I was running as fast as I could but I was pretty buzzed and couldn't tell if I was really running as fast as I thought I was. But I kept going. I kept telling myself, *You're lightning, Missy. You are fucking lightning.* I could feel something clanking in my backpack. It was two bottled beers that I forgot were in there and being the fucking drunk I was, I actually had to take a moment to consider whether or not I should throw one at them because I didn't wanna waste my beers on those fucks and I knew if I survived this harrowing experience I was gonna need a fucking beer. Again with the fucking Catch-22.

I felt my chest hurt and I was out of breath. I could see the Boardwalk ahead and then I heard Hector yell.

"Fucking scatter!"

Hector took off on my right and Angie on my left and I just kept running dead-ahead. I could still hear someone chasing me but I wasn't sure and I was too afraid to turn around and look so I ran up onto the boardwalk where all the people were and ducked into the crowd. I made it towards a public restroom and ran inside, ran into an empty stall, and slammed the door. There were other women and children in there so I thought I would be okay. I don't know how long I waited, but it must have been awhile because a knock on the stall door came and an elderly lady asked if I was alright. I told her I just went on a ride and felt sick, but that I would be okay.

I left the restroom and just as I looked right, I saw one of the Nazis looking around, looking for me. I ducked into the crowd again, and made it under the boardwalk, hiding in a corner. It smelled so fucking bad down there and I was worried that something happened to Angie or Hector. And it was getting dark. I waited for at least thirty minutes down there until I heard a faint whistle. I knew that sound. It was Juan.

"Hey, you okay?" He had some blood coming from his mouth and his hands were all kinds of bruised but he looked okay for the most part.

"I am so fucking glad to see you," I said throwing my arms around him. I couldn't help it. I had to hug him because I was so relieved to be alive and if he was okay, chances were all of us were okay.

"We gotta get back to Watsonville, chica. The hotel called the cops and I can't be getting caught up."

"Is everyone okay?" I asked.

"Yeah—Mario got his nose busted but he's cool. That was the worst of it. As soon as those fuckers came up on us a bunch of workers that stay at the hotel came out and helped us handle it. But I think you should get back to the school and we'll get back to Watsonville. I'll walk you to the bus."

I got back to my room at the school that night and called Juan's house.

"Look, it's nothing personal, but we gotta cool it for a bit. You know, kicking it. Me, Mario all of us—we're family so we know we can handle ourselves. But with you it's different. You're hella cool Missy, don't get me wrong. It's just how things gotta be right now."

"Yeah, I understand."

I hung up the phone, fell back on my bed, stared at the ceiling, alone. Again.

IN REGARDS TO ANARCHY

It was a week after being chased by the skins. I decided that Santa Cruz was a pile of shit and that this whole college experiment was a big waste of my time. I was supposed to be in Seattle anyways. I was supposed to be in a band like Mia Zapata. But being smart fucked all my punk rock plans. And Ricky going to prison. And my sister, Espi, getting pregnant...again. And Nesto. Well my other brother, Nesto, didn't really do nothing. And doing nothing is its own stupid-ass problem. So my parents laid this whole trip on me. I was supposed to be in a big, burgeoning scene—not being held up by knife point and chased down by neo-Nazis. I was supposed to be in college. Really be in college. I wanted to dedicate myself, but the truth of the matter was that the school was also full of crazy white people, the forest, the dark—it gets so dark in the forest. After being there almost six weeks I was still stripping in the city on weekends. I thought I'd go norms and get a job at some coffee shop or restaurant. But every time I would leave the end of my shift I felt cheated. I mean, I was pulling

17

my same moves there to get tips that I was stripping at Michelle's XXX back in LA and making far less money. That's really the kicker—the money. Don't let no one tell you different. Oh, I'm sure there's lots of girls who say they do it for a million other reasons but I'm not one of them. I'm a shallow, get-rich-quick kind of bitch and if dumb motherfuckers want my attention, they're gonna have to pay for it. It's as simple as that.

I was walking down Pacific Avenue when I was going over all of these deep thoughts, when a scraggly white girl with a fucked-up Mohawk stumbled towards me. Now, when I say a fucked-up Mohawk I'm not playin' with you—I mean FUCKED-UP. Like it was lop-sided and cut by a three-year-old. This chick stumbles towards me and she's like, "What's your name?"

And I don't know—something in me finally snapped. Maybe it was the situation with the skins the week before. Maybe it was all the fuckin', rich hippies at college driving BMWs but don't seem to have enough money to wash their clothes or take a bath. Maybe it was just being four-hundred miles away from the neighborhood, from dark faces, and all the realness I'd come to know as the only way to be "down." I can't tell you. Alls I know is that The Me, the real me, just came out and in all my straight-up LA-Mexican-head-swingin'-chola/tough-bitch-of-a-girl-attitude I said, two inches from her face, "What's your name?"

She took a step back and just looked at me. Then she smiled.

"I like you," she said.

And thus began my friendship with one Anarchy Romeo.

Anarchy was my true introduction to gutter punx. She had a squat underneath the San Lorenzo Bridge in the park behind the main downtown area. It was very organized and pretty quiet over there. She managed to rig up a series of water-proof tents with some phone cord and a series of well-tied sailor knots. It looked like a kid's fort or club house but once you stepped inside, it was a nice place to live. She even had cable TV. I spent much of my time there and to be honest, we didn't always sit around and talk. We would just sit. And I liked that. I was sick of the stupid college routine where you always had to come up with something brilliant and/or funny and/or interesting to say. That shit was a mask. I was raised in a family where it was okay to be quiet, and sometimes necessary because my Pop worked nights and slept during the day.

"Do you want some?" Anarchy asked, passing me some kind of crushed powder.

"No, I can't—we get drug tested because of the scholarship."

"Oh."

Then she'd snort it—whatever it was. And we'd keep sitting.

"So I was thinking...you still wanna score some money?"

"Yeah, I need to. You're not gonna make me steal, are you?"

"Since when do I steal?" she said.

She was right—she never had to steal. She just had this way of getting what she wanted. She was always smiling and nice to people and they never saw that coming from a girl like her. It was hard to say no to a smiling spanger. And men. There was this mystery she had with men. They would just give her shit without expecting anything. I know it sounds too good to be true, but I'd been friends with her for almost a month, practically held up in that squat with her and there it would be—a bottle of Jaeger, drugs, clothes, smokes, food, a twenty dollar bill. These dudes—okay, men. Like the kind of men that come to the club—suits. Straight up suits—would come down to the squat and they'd bring stuff by, and talk for awhile, and then leave. Until next time.

"So, what is it? What's the gig?" I asked.

She took a drag off a cigarette.

"So, there's this guy. In the Santa Cruz mountains. And he's got a really nice pad, okay? I mean, really nice. He's come by once…I think you were here—well anyway, he knows I'm trying to get the fuck out of here. I gotta get to Seattle. You 'member how I told you that I was supposed to be in Seattle, like, a year ago? I've still been tryin' to make it back."

"So why don't you? I've seen the twenty dollar bills and the drugs girl…"

"That's just it—I can't find this kind of action anywhere else, you know? So, going to Seattle is kind of like you going to college. I gotta *do* something."

"So, what you gotta do? At the guy's house?"

"He just wants me and another girl to make-out, naked, for like, two hours. No touching him, no photos. He just wants to watch."

I rolled my eyes, because that's what these fucks always say. And it doesn't matter whether they're men or women. My last call like this was in the Hollywood

Hills somewhere about eight months ago. This woman came to the club and invited me back to her house for an extra two-hundred dollars and of course I went and of course I thought it was okay because she wasn't bigger than me and I was pretty sure I could take her if I had to. But we got there, and it wasn't a private dance it's sex and asphyxiation and I went along with it but she didn't know what she was doing and I almost choked to death. And she felt really bad for doing it wrong and gave me an extra hundred dollars and a ride back to my girlfriend's house. You'd think that would scare me straight but it didn't—I just remembered to never let them touch my throat like that again.

Anarchy kept smoking.

"Look, it's not like the Hills dude…"

Did I mention she was creepily psychic? Either that, or she was a real good listener.

"It's not like that at all. I've hung out with this guy a lot and he's one of those hippie, tantra, Baba dudes. They think it's all spiritual. You know—like paying for this type of stuff isn't prostitution because they're on some high, spiritual trip and doing it for spiritual reasons. Like they're giving money to a church or guru or something. And besides, it's five-hundred dollars."

"Five-hundred dollars?"

"Yup. That's two-fifty each, for two hours, with no sex. I know we're just friends but, I don't really know any other girls and besides—I figure kissing you is okay."

On Saturday we went to the mountains.

I hadn't been to the mountains before. Except in Mexico. But in Santa Cruz, it's more forest—a shit ton

21

more forest. Okay, you're probably wondering why I have such a trip on the forest. The truth is—I'm scared. Look, I know usually it's the "big city" that scares people. With the noise, lights, and violence. But at least you know people are around. You know, civilization? The only time I'd ever seen the forest was in horror movies like *Friday the 13th*. And *Halloween*. Okay, *Halloween* doesn't really take place in the forest but every time I have to walk through the college at night that song, "Da da dum da da dum..." runs through my head and I can't think straight. My condition with going to this Baba Whatever's house was that it be during the afternoon, during daylight. I was not about to get stuck up at that place at night, no fucking way.

The bus dropped us off at the base of the mountain which is more like a giant hill. We walked up, through trees, so many trees, along this bike path. Finally, we reached a small clearing and as we walked through it, there was Baba Whatever's house. Anarchy was right—it was amazing. Huge. Like a giant tree house with lots of windows. I imagine that I will have to come to terms with nature because this is probably what the future is going to look like after the revolution.

"You want some of this before we go in?" Anarchy said, showing me some pills.

"Okay." Fuck the scholarship.

Anarchy crushed the pills really fine with the butt-end of her knife, then she took out a straw, and we shot. It was a straight shot up my nose and I was thankful because I couldn't get too fucked up by trying to shoot more than once.

"What exactly is this guy's name anyway?" I asked.

"I think it's Ed. But he wants us to refer to him by his Baba name."

"What? What's that?"

"Baba Goree."

"You're fuckin' jokin', right?"

"I told you—it's all tantra, spiritual shit."

I wasn't sure I could keep a straight face calling him that. But for two-hundred and fifty bucks I was willing to go the extra mile.

We rang the doorbell, which sounded like a gong. Then a fairly well-built man in a skirt-like-thing and long brown hair, and a modest goatee came to the door. He just stood there for a second, smiling and looking at us. Anarchy gladly smiled but I wasn't sure what to do. Then he put his hands together in front of him like he was going to pray.

"Namaste," he said.

"Namaste," Anarchy said.

We went inside. Baba Goree took us to the back of the house, to a giant, open room with all kinds of statues and flowers. I think the statues were from India. The entire back wall wasn't a wall at all but a giant window, and all I could see was trees. He didn't ask my name or even call Anarchy by hers, which was fine by me.

"This is where we will be practicing today. Do the two of you ever dabble in gem lore?"

"In gem what?" I asked.

"Gem lore. It's the study of gems and how they affect your life."

When Baba Goree spoke his voice was slow and breathy—like a tantric Marilyn Monroe or a fucked-up open mic. Every word was pronounced with each syllable like the act of talking itself was sex. It would have been sexy, but this was work so it was just weird. And he was weird. And... fuck—I was just a Chicana from South Central LA so everything was either weird and/or strange to me.

"I've picked out some sacred gems that I think will help us on this journey today."

"And, what is our journey today?" I asked.

He just smiled. And then began to take off his skirt thing.

"Wait a minute...what the fuck do you think you're doing?"

"Oh, don't worry Lakasha—I'm only allowing my vessel to be in its natural state."

"Lakasha?" I said, my eyebrow raised.

"Yes, you are Lakasha. I've met you in a past life. You're a great communicator, diplomat, and artist from 840 BCE. I knew we had met before when I looked into your eyes back at the front entrance. But that was many lifetimes ago—you probably don't remember now."

"Yeah, she has a bad memory for past lives Baba," Anarchy chimed in.

Anarchy and I took off our clothes and Baba sat cross-legged towards the back of the room with his eyes closed. We sat there for what felt like a million more lifetimes.

"I'm now in-touch with you...you can begin..." Baba said finally.

Anarchy turned to me, and it occurred to me that it was the first time I'd ever seen her naked before. She was beautiful. Stunning actually. It was the first time since we'd met that she really looked into my eyes. Except for that time I got kicked out of that straight-edge show at the Vets Hall for arriving drunk and then projectile vomiting onto the security guard, then the last thing I remembered was waking up in the park near her squat the next morning with Anarchy leaning over me, looking me in the eyes.

"You are so awesome and inappropriate," she said.

But since then, never. She leaned in slow and began kissing me. Her mouth felt good, and she turned out to be a good kisser. She kept kissing me and I realized I hadn't been kissed since NaTanya, the love of my life, broke-up with me. It had been four long months of my mouth hitting bottles and making a pout that I almost forgot how good it felt to be kissing. Anarchy put her hand around the back of my head and pulled me in, kissing me more intensely and I could feel my body responding to her control of the situation.

"Yes, I can feel the energy you are sending out, Lakasha, to Tryndesa—it's so powerful…" Baba Goree's voice came in, his eyes still closed.

Then he started to sway a little from side to side. Anarchy kept kissing me until I finally accepted that this was really happening and I kissed her back. She seemed surprised and actually giggled a little. I kissed her some more and I pushed her hand away from my head and then pushed her down on the floor, straddling her and holding her down with her arms outstretched. I began to grind my clit against her pussy and forced my mouth on her so intensely that at times she couldn't breathe.

"Do that again," she whispered in my ear.

And I did. I kept going until out-of-nowhere she picked me up and body-slammed me down on the hardwood floor, her forearm at my throat while her other arm held my thigh down. She had her mouth at my cunt but she wouldn't taste it—just kept blowing hot hair from her mouth onto my shaved pussy, making me crazy. And then Baba Goree's swaying became stronger and his voice louder and less breathy.

"YES! Keep going! The energy of the gods is immense right now! I sense the two of you are working out an ancient conflict! Karma has finally come to take what's hers!"

He started chanting, like those people who speak in tongues or some shit. Anarchy kept holding me down and the harder she held me the more I could feel myself surrender to her. I didn't want to fight her. I wanted her to go harder, rougher. And I don't know if it was all that hot air on my pussy she was givin' me but the fact that she wouldn't touch me down there made me a little pissed off. And I suddenly found my knee kick her in the stomach. She flew a few feet away from me and sat there for a moment, a little dumb. Then she caught her breath and came at me, knocked me down, sending me back against some of the sacred gems Baba Goree had placed on the floor. Then we were full on wrestling, using all of our strength. It happened so fast. And Baba Goree kept rocking and yelling.

"THE BALANCE OF CREATION IS CALLING! The forces of nature have all risen to meet us at our historic feast! YES! YES! GIVE BIRTH TO EACH OTHER!"

Then I slapped her, and she slapped me back. It stung and my reflexes gave through to a punch to the right side of her face. Her lip was bleeding. We stopped for a moment. She took some of the blood from her lip, stood up, and rubbed it across her chest. She then got on all fours and crawled towards me. I was ready for her to fuckin' kick my ass. But instead, when she reached me, she took my face in her hands and kissed me, very sweetly. She kissed me again and again and we went back to making out. Then she sat back on the floor and pulled me on top of her. We were directly in front of Baba Goree who was crying and the two of us just kept touching each other and kissing and then she looked at me again, or she looked *into* me. We just looked at each other for awhile, while she put her hand on my heart and then took my hand and put it on hers. Then it got quiet. Real quiet. After a few more lifetimes, Baba Goree finally stopped rocking and returned to just sitting, being still. Then he opened his eyes.

"Thank you Lakasha and Tryndesa—thank you for letting me bare witness to your ancient struggle. I feel that your past lives are finally at peace. This has been a good practice," he said in his original tantra voice.

Baba Goree got up, put his skirt-thing back on, and invited us to dress our vessels. We cleaned up in the bathroom. He walked us to the door again, gave us the money, and gave us the gems from the sacred room.

"To remember what you have done today," he said.

He shut the door. We walked down the mountain, not speaking. I put my gem in my pocket so I wouldn't lose it—I decided I never wanted to lose it. Anarchy took hers and threw it into the forest.

"Why'd you do that?" I said.

"It's just glass. Don't worry, it's not worth anything," she smiled.

"Don't you wanna keep it?"

"Why? It's just some glass from some guy. I know another guy we can do this routine with…" she said.

I was walking ahead, making sure she didn't see I cared.

FOSSILS

Anarchy and I became a tag-team act. A dirty, fucked-up duet. She knew more Babas. Lots more. Santa Cruz was apparently full of Baba dudes and they were all willing to pay top dollar for our act.

"Dude—I thought you were really gonna knock my tooth out that time!" Anarchy chuckled, as we slid down the side of Highway 17 fresh from another successful act.

"Don't tempt me," I said, annoyed.

"What the hell is your problem?" she sneered.

"Nothing."

We continued sliding down the hill, several steps in front of each other. After pulling these hustles, I realized that something was happening to me. Each time I locked eyes with her I was giving something away. At first, I didn't know how to feel about it. It was just a hustle. A gig. Work. But lately, it felt different.

"Hey, can you slow the fuck down?" Anarchy shouted to me.

"Why don't you speed the fuck up?" I said.

She finally caught up to me at the bottom of the hill, walking up the side of the highway.

"Look, you're being a real fuckin' bitch right now..." she began, a little hazy.

I knew she had been doing heroin. I saw her works at the squat earlier. And I knew it was probably the heroin that thought I was a fuckin' bitch. Anarchy never got mad at me, never got mad at anyone. I'd never even heard her raise her voice before now.

"What?" I said.

"You know what—you're being such a fuckin' baby right now."

"Really, that's how I'm being? I guess you know everything don't you?"

"I know a fuckin' jealous person when I see one," she said.

"Jealous?"

"Yeah—you're jealous that these Baba dudes want me all the time. You're jealous 'cuz you know that if it wasn't for me, you wouldn't even have this gig."

"Are you fucking *serious*?!" I shouted.

I walked ahead. Faster. Away from her. What a fucking drug addict. To think that I was jealous of the attention these fucks were giving her! It was unbelievable.

"You are so fuckin' delusional!" I shouted.

"It's true isn't it? Well, you know what—fine then. Fuck you. Be a jealous whore!"

She pushed me. I pushed her back. She pushed me again. Then I pushed her hard and she lost her footing, and fell against some rocks, her face hitting the pavement. There was blood, lots of blood, from her mouth. Then she held up her hand, with what looked like a tiny white pebble in it and smiled at me.

"You did it—you finally did it. You knocked that fuckin' tooth out of me."

I got down on the ground beside her.

"I'm sorry—I'm so sorry. I didn't mean to do that," I pleaded.

Then she kissed me. She kissed me so soft, just like we always did at the end of a hustle.

"Don't, don't..." I whispered.

She kept kissing me, the taste of her blood in my mouth like a sweet medicine. I kept kissing her 'til I fell on top of her and we just made-out, right there on the side of the highway, only a few speeding cars passing. I could see the light fading through the trees. It was gonna be dark soon, and we were still three miles from the squat.

"Stop it, just let go for once. Stop thinking," she said, pulling my face back to meet hers.

"I'm so tired of thinking..." I said.

Anarchy pulled a small bottle of pills out of her pocket, sat up, and started crushing them with her knife. She passed me the powder and a straw.

"Here, let's just be here right now."

I shot. It was a straight-shoot. I laid in the dirt and leaves, next to her. I was chasing the shadows above me with every slow breath. Anarchy huddled against me. Her swollen mouth was pulsing against my neck while we wrapped ourselves around each other.

It was dawn when I woke-up. I looked down and I was alone. I sat up quick and realized what a stupid move that was, since it made me dizzy as fuck. I looked at my watch. 6am. I kept rubbing my eyes, almost in disbelief that I not only spent the night in the scary-ass forest but that I was alone, too.

"Hey," Anarchy said, coming up behind me.

"Fuck, girl—I thought you left me here."

"Since when do I leave you anywhere? Come on. I know a place we can get some free food," she smiled.

I got up and we walked. We did what we always did, walk and not speak. This happened after every hustle, the morning after every punk show or all night binge. It's the unspoken moment of silence amongst thieves.

After about an hour and fifteen minutes, we reached downtown. I was starving, remembering that I hadn't eaten since the afternoon before. We walked to the backdoor of a bagel shop. One of the suits that comes by the squat saw us through the screen door.

"Hey Ted—got anything for us to eat?"

"Just… stay here," Ted said.

We waited about five minutes and he came back with a brown paper bag.

"You gotta get out of here, Jenny. I'll try to come by and check on you later," Ted said.

We took the bag to the squat. It was full of bagels, some cream cheese, and juice. We ate. And again it was silent. Anarchy pulled some cash out of her pocket and handed me some crumpled bills.

"These are yours."

"Your real name is Jenny?" I asked.

"Sometimes," she replied.

"When?"

"When I feel like it. When guys like Ted are real nice to me and don't expect anything. Then. That's when my name is Jenny."

We kept eating. I didn't even know what day it was, but I had a sneaking suspicion that I was supposed to be getting ready to go to the city and dance later that night.

"You gotta go. It's Friday," Anarchy said.

"Yeah. I do."

"Here—it's yours. You earned it." She handed me her tooth with a crooked smile on her face.

"I can't take that…"

"Why, does it gross you out?"

"A little—well, it's weird—"

"Everything about me is weird, Missy, duh. Please. You're the one that rattled it loose in the first place—you have a mean right-hook," she laughed.

"Okay."

I put the tooth in my pocket.

"See you when I get back, 'kay?"

Anarchy just sat there, her back to me, smoking a cigarette.

Monday came, and I got into Santa Cruz late morning. I didn't have a class until the afternoon, so I quickly headed over to the squat to see Anarchy. I managed to make a little extra money and thought we could go spend it at the liquor store. But when I reached the bridge, it was empty. The squat was gone. There was just one tarp and some rope hanging off the side of the bridge, the wind blowing it gently towards the sky. I stood for a minute, confused. My first instinct was that the cops came by and picked her up for squatting or drugs or some bullshit. I went back to Pacific Avenue to the Metro Station where a lot of the gutter punx and homeless kids hung out. I saw Bob, one of the punx that I met through Anarchy.

"Hey dude, you seen Anarchy around?"

"No, no man—she's gone."

"What? Did she get arrested or something?"

"No, no nothing like that—she bailed. We smoked some shit and then she got on a greyhound."

"When?"

"I don't know—a few days ago? Something like that. Hey, Missy—do you have fifty cents? Or a dollar? I really need to get to Natural Bridges…"

"Yeah, yeah man."

I gave Bob some money, a couple bucks. Then I walked back to the bridge. There was no note. No sign that she'd ever really been there. I just sat there, listening to the people walking across the boards above me. I didn't cry. I didn't feel anything. I opened the pocket of my jean jacket. I pulled out Anarchy's tooth. It was still pretty white, considering I never saw her brush her teeth. It sparkled a little against the mid-morning sun. I held it in my hand, the only proof I had that any of the last few weeks even existed. Then I dug up some loose dirt and buried it. A small grave. Then I walked.

CHOLOS, BIG BROTHERS, AND LOVEY-DOVEY SHIT

After hearing Anarchy got on the bus to Seattle, I felt a knot in my stomach I didn't expect. To say things ended kinda messy wasn't accurate because I wasn't sure if they fuckin' ever began. Anyways, I knew that she was gone. And I was back to being on my own.

I started going to the city even when I wasn't dancing at Harry's. I would go to shows and it seemed like nobody even cared I was there and it was great. I hung out with JB a lot. He had pretty much adopted me as his "little sister" and it made it so easy to just make friends and get into pretty much any club I wanted. It was almost surreal, you know? Knowing a punk legend and actually having him look out for you. The only problem? Getting one of these types to take you on as a "big brother" pretty much made you un-fuckable to much of the punk-rock population. No guy would fuckin' touch me for fear that they might fuck me over and get ejected from the scene, and trust me at this time in the 90s that was worse than getting your ass kicked. Though that was a good reason too. To have

35

a famous punk as a big-brother basically meant I was resigned to only fucking girls which was fine by me. Until Carlos.

Carlos was actually a friend of Ricky's, my real older brother. He was friends with both my brothers and much of my neighborhood, even though he was in Watts and we were in South Central. Carlos just finished serving five years in San Quinten and had some cousins in Watsonville and a hip, gay uncle in San Francisco. He decided that staying out just might be a good idea, since much of the old neighborhood was either dead, locked up, or just lost. There was nothing left in LA for him, I supposed.

Carlos got my digits from JB and called me up. Now before I go into this phone call, lemme tell you a little more about this homie. He was about ten years older than me, a definite man not a kid. A really hot man. The truth is, he was this straight-up vato—I mean as cholo as they get. But he loved punk-rock. And he loved punk girls. I remember right before he got locked up I was thirteen and I just started going to punk shows with Espi, my sister. Here's the thing about Mexicans: as long as you have an older sibling or cousin or tio or tia, you are pretty much allowed to go anywhere and do just about anything. Espi wasn't really into punk but I desperately wanted to go to shows and she loved me so she went. I remember seeing Carlos there and being totally fucking confused. I mean, he'd be there in his creased Ben Davis, cortez's, white t-shirt, gang tattoos, slicked black hair, Tres Flores and he'd just be kickin' it with these full on punk dudes and hanging out. Anyways, it wasn't long before we all found out about him getting locked up and I would hear things about him here and there from my brothers and his sister who was my age and went to school with me. I never really thought of Carlos as anything but just Carlos from the neighborhood until I heard he was out of prison and living with his uncle in the Mission about four blocks from me and JB.

JB gave him our number, probably thinking we were just old friends and shit. So, Carlos called me up.

"Hey guerita…it's me Carlos. I don't even know if you remember me, girl! It's been a long time and heard you were around. So…hi. And…maybe I'll see you around. Late," said the message he left on JB's answering machine.

JB encouraged me to hang out with him since I didn't feel like I had anyone I could talk to about stuff besides him and I think he was tired of hearing about Anarchy so much.

"Just fuckin' talk to him at the show tonight. You need a friend dude. Like a friend. That's not me. That's not a fucked up squatter from Santa Cruz who left your ass without even saying good-bye," JB said.

So, I did talk to Carlos at JB's show. It wasn't even awkward. Kind of like talking to my own brothers for a second. He still looked the same, only older and with a mustache and goatee now and a shaved head. He still looked hard, worn even. Getting locked-up does that shit to you. My brother looked the same way last time I saw him. I told Carlos he still wasn't out yet but that next time I wrote him I would tell him about us meeting up in of all places, Frisco.

"You look…really different…" he said.

"Like how?"

"Like…different," he said. Then he smiled and something kind of happened in me. I felt that same stupid knot I felt for Anarchy and it was huge, I mean fucking overwhelming.

"Well…the last time you saw me I was just a kid. I was thirteen."

"And now?" he said.

"Now I'm not," I replied.

And he smiled again. And I smiled. We started spending a lot of time together.

JB was glad that I wasn't a cranky mess anymore. He kept telling me to snap out of it or else I wouldn't make any money at Harry's and then I'd be even more depressed.

"No one likes a mopey stripper, baby. Not even one as cute as you."

I think it also gave JB piece-of-mind to know I wasn't out hooking up with endless guys in the scene, worrying his ass to death. He was always worried about me. I mean, he really took this whole older brother thing seriously. He would always tell me how punk guys can suck and treat chicks like shit and how he should know because he is one. And that's why he wasn't dating right now, just in a band, just touring, whatever. And me being eighteen and a stripper moonlighting as a normal college student just made him even more fuckin' worried that one of these dudes would just fucking clean me out or fuck me over in a serious way and how it would become his problem because he'd have to kick the guy's ass or something like that. Being with Carlos was actually pretty relieving. I mean, JB was rad but being with Carlos was kind of like my little piece of home here in the city. Carlos' uncle got him a job at this late-night diner in the Castro as a line-cook and after he got off work he'd come over to Harry's and bring me eggs and toast and hang out with me on my break out behind the club. I don't know exactly when things changed between us, I just remember that one night I met Carlos at his job and we walked back to his uncle's place.

"You know, my tio's out of town…" he said.

"Okay…"

"Do you wanna come up for awhile?"

"Maybe I should get back to JB's. I still have a paper I'm supposed to be working on…"

He took my hand and we stood under a lamp in the dirty street, the evening fog falling over me like tiny comets.

"What if I say 'please'?" he said.

"What if you do?"

He licked his lips and leaned in. The kiss was good. Really good. Like when I kissed NaTanya, my first real girlfriend, for the first time. The knot in my stomach was just gone and I felt totally dizzy and stupid and filled with heat. Before I knew it I was practically racing him up the stairs to his uncle's third floor apartment and I couldn't get my clothes off fast enough.

"We can't tell JB about this, okay?" I said.

"Why not?" he said, laying on top of me, kissing me so good around my ear and my most favorite part of my neck.

"Cuz. He doesn't want me to hook-up with dudes in the scene and all. And I'm staying at his place so I can't afford to fuck that up. So, just don't say nothing okay?"

He looked into me with the most amazing brown eyes, then he took his hand and ran it across my face.

"Okay, quierda. I won't say nothing."

Even though he wasn't the first dude I had sex with I decided that he was because the other dudes—well let's just say it wasn't sex. I never said no but then again, I never said yes. This time all I could manage to say was *yes, more, harder, faster, please, fuck, god damn, yesyesyes. Yes…*

The next morning I woke-up and dressed, all in silence. I didn't wanna wake Carlos and I needed to get back to JB's fast before he got back and wondered where the hell I'd been all night. I stood in the front doorway and I heard a voice.

"So, that's how it's gonna be?"

It was Carlos in just his chinos, lighting a cigarette.

"I'm sorry, I just really have to get back…"

He walked toward me.

"It's okay. But don't treat me like those other dudes, okay? Don't treat me like a john."

"You're not. I wasn't…" I said.

He pulled me into him and kissed me and then he just held me there for awhile.

"Just stand here for a minute, okay? I just wanna smell you a little longer…"

He buried his face into my neck and breathed deep. I could feel my entire body melt into him, into the hardwood floor, and I got that dizzy-stupid thing again.

"Okay, will you call me? Tonight? After you get off work? Can I meet you later?" he said, looking at me.

"Yeah. Yes. I will call you and I'll see you tonight."

"I miss you already, mamita."

"Okay," I said, and ran back to JB's house.

Ten minutes after I got to the apartment JB and the guys rolled up in the van, makin' all kinds of noise outside. I pretended to be in my room working on that stupid Shakespeare paper when really, I could still smell Carlos in-between my fingers and the wetness between my legs was so intense—I wished I could just go back over to his uncle's and get on top of him again, my body riding high on him, bouncing all over the place as he held me up and kept saying all those sweet things NaTanya used to say to me, while thrusting deeper and deeper into me.

"What the fuck up, kitten?" JB said.

"Not much brother. Just homework."

"Good girl. Hey I'm gonna go out tonight and probably stay in Oakland with those fuckers. You cool? I know you work and then go to the Cruz later. You alright being here alone again?"

"Yeah, yeah totally."

"Great."

Then he left. And I called Carlos.

SEX, LIES, AND PUNK ROCK

In less than an hour, Carlos was at JB's place and we picked up where we left off the night before. Before I knew it, almost a month had passed and I could feel myself getting into something but I didn't care. Carlos was home to me and as much as I didn't want to admit it, I was homesick. I missed seeing familiar faces, the safe routines I created, even my dad's smile. And my brother. He was still in County after almost eight months and as his trial date approached, it didn't look good. For the first time since I landed here I felt selfish. I was the first to go to college, get a scholarship, actually do something with my fuckin' self and I was dancing at the TGIFriday's of strip clubs, getting drunk, and secretly fooling around with one of my brother's friends zip codes away. I was seriously ridiculous.

"What's wrong?" Carlos said on top of me. I had gotten lost in my own head that I almost forgot I was supposed to be having sex.

"Nothing. Sorry."

He got off of me.

"What's up with you? You've been acting really… different. Are you fucking some other dude?" he said.

"No, that you don't have to worry about," I replied firmly.

"Then what? Are you fucking up? In trouble?"

"No, no it's not that…"

He put his pants on, sat at the foot of my tiny twin bed, and lit a cigarette.

"Then let's go out tonight—let's go to a show together," he said.

"I can't—I think I need to head back to school later."

He looked down and exhaled. Hard.

"Seriously, what the fuck is going on?" he pressed.

"I don't know what you're talking about."

I got up quickly and went into the bathroom. I tried to look in the small, dirty mirror but I couldn't find any answers. Carlos opened the door.

"Look, I'm not tryin' to sound like a whiny bitch but I feel like you're embarrassed to be with me or something."

"It's not that…"

"Well then what's up? We've been doing this shit for about a month now and you still won't be seen with me. You always bounce after we have sex and every time I ask you to go to a show or something you always got some shit to do. I mean I know you're a college-girl and all but, I don't get it. It doesn't feel right."

I could see his face in the mirror's reflection. He looked vulnerable, like he cared. But I couldn't get the words out.

"You know what then, I'll see you later," he said.

He got dressed and left, slamming the front door to the apartment. I just kept standing in the bathroom bracing myself with the sink. Another voice came barreling into the fuckin' space.

"What's up kitten?!"

It was JB. Great.

"I'm in the bathroom!" I yelled.

"Well I'll talk to you through the door. So, I'm fuckin' stoked because the band just booked a three week tour and the piece-of-shit label we're on is actually gonna foot the bill. It's like I won the punk-rock lottery or something."

I opened the door.

"That's great JB. Fucking awesome."

I moved past him into the make-shift living room, pulled up a milk crate, and sat down pretending to rustle some papers and look busy.

"Hey I saw Carlos cut out of here pretty fast—he running late again?"

"Yeah, you know how it is."

"You're not fuckin' with him are you?"

I froze. Fuck, I was so obvious.

"What do you mean?" I said.

I looked down at my feet, always my feet. The ground, always the ground. I wanted to dig a nice warm hole and crawl inside. JB just stood there staring at me, up and down.

"Nah! You're into girls and thank goddess for that," he joked.

"Yup, I'm into girls."

"And it's a good thing because I would definitely lose it if you were fooling around with these fuckin' clowns."

I realized that my secrets wouldn't be secrets for long. So I did what anyone who is leading multiple lives would do: I got defensive and picked a fight with him.

"You know JB, you can be seriously judgmental."

"What?"

"Yeah dude, you are. You are so fucking judgmental. You act like you know everything and you're better than everyone else because you've been around for a million years and seriously, there's a word for that: arrogant."

"Oh really, where did you learn that big word? College? Oh that's right—you're in college but don't give a fuck and I guess for you that's so cool. You're so Generation X. Way to fucking go," he snapped back.

"You know what? I *am* in college and don't give a fuck but at least I admit it. I make my stupid mistakes and move on. I don't go around telling you who you can talk to or fuck or whatever…"

"Yeah you really admit it by running away to the city every week and hiding in my closet and getting fucked up on whatever you can get your hands on."

"Yeah well it's just one more thing you can tell me is wrong with me, JB. You can add it to your brotherly, over-protective list of things that are fucking wrong with me…"

"You've got to be fucking kidding me—" he said, and then stopped. He looked right at me, with a half-smile of disbelief.

"You're fucking Carlos," he said.

"No I'm not," I said.

"Yes, yes you are—this is exactly what this is about. You're fucking that guy. And you kinda like him."

"That's not what's fucking going on!" I yelled.

I realized that this strategy of picking a fight was going south. Fast. I was being cornered.

"You are fucking Carlos! You totally are and I can't believe I didn't see it until now. You lied to me!" he yelled.

"I didn't lie to you. I just didn't tell you the whole truth."

"That's a fucking lie, Missy. Have you two been going at it in my apartment?"

"Look I pay rent too—if I wanna do shit like that here I should be able to."

"Wow, you are someone I don't know. You are a fucking stranger to me right now. Who the fuck are you?" he said.

"I'm *me* motherfucker! I'm good ol' fucked up *me* and it's about time you saw all of my rainbow of shitty colors because there's a lot you don't fucking know about me!" I screamed.

"That's clear. Do you know that he has kids? *Kids,* Missy. He has two kids and he's still with the mom. He's way still with the mom. So now you're a fucking homewrecker. You're the other woman. And you aren't even into guys—this is fucking amazing right now..."

"He never told me nothing about no kids or girl—"

"Of course he's not gonna tell you Missy! He's a fucking guy! He's a punk guy! A punk, cholo guy who just got out of prison and is hella older than you. What do you think guys like that are looking for in an eighteen-year-old pole-dancer? You really think it's your brain that turns him on?"

"You don't know what we talk about, how we are—you don't fucking know anything."

"I know that if you fuck him in my house, even one more time, you and I are seriously gonna have a problem. I mean a real fucking problem."

"Fine!" I shouted and then slammed the door to what was supposed to be my room. I heard the front door slam. And there it was. It was finally all out there. I knew JB would be back later and I knew that I was sick of his shit, everyone's shit—all people ever wanted to do was control me and I was done. If I wasn't on a good one before I was definitely headed for one now. And I was gonna start by calling Carlos one more time.

REVENGE OR SOMETHING LIKE THAT

Carlos wanted to talk, but I had other things on mind. I was definitely going to let JB know that he was not my parents, not the boss of my shit. I heard JB stumble back into the apartment about an hour earlier and I was pretty sure he was passed out on his bed but I was still going to go through with my plan.

"Hey," Carlos said at the front door.

"Quick, get in here."

I pulled him into the apartment and kissed him. He put his arms around me and his mouth was so warm.

"Let's go into my room," I whispered.

I started tearing his clothes off and before he could say a word I pushed him onto my bed and got on top.

"Why are you in such a hurry, girl?" Carlos said playfully.

"I'm not in a hurry—just excited."

We kept making-out and I could hear some movement in JB's room through the thin wall that separated our spaces. I took my pants off and kept grinding on top of Carlos. I started moaning loudly..

"Oh, Carlos—oh yeah papa, yeah give it to me…"

"Don't you think we should keep it down baby? I think JB is home," Carlos whispered.

"Oh I don't think he's here—just keep going," I told him.

We kept going at it and it was clear I was going to need to make more noise. I kept moaning louder and louder until I was almost yelling.

"YES! YES! OH YES!"

I could hear JB in his room. He turned his stereo on. But that just encouraged me to be even louder.

"YEEESSSSSS! OH MY GOD! FUCK! YEAH, THAT'S WHAT I LIKE!"

"Damn baby, I've never seen you like this before," Carlos said in my ear.

"You can keep up right?" I said coyly.

Carlos was completely going for it. I was bouncing on top of him, moaning and yelling my ass off. JB turned the stereo up more. I started banging the thin wall between us all the while still yelling.

"YES! YES! RIGHT THERE!"

Bang, bang, bang with my right fist. Finally I could hear the stereo being turned off. Then two doors slam. JB was gone. Good. Point made.

I got off of Carlos and quickly stood up and put my pants back on. I sat on the bed and lit a cigarette.

"What the fuck baby—what's wrong? Why are we stopping?" Carlos said.

"I just need a break," I replied.

Carlos lay there for a minute, staring at the ceiling. I smoked in silence.

"Look, I'm no fucking piece of shit, Missy. I know I've been fucked up but not in a long time and especially not with you."

"I don't know what you're talking about dude," I whined.

"Are you gonna be my girl or what?"

"Carlos—"

"I...love you," he said looking down.

And there it was. The truth. But being me I couldn't handle it. I cared about Carlos but I knew that JB was right: I'm mainly into girls. I knew this, ran away to be this, and deep down I always knew that someday, somehow I would end up with a woman. And I was eighteen anyways. I wasn't a woman yet, no matter what anyone said. I was in over my head, not the first time, but this time I was gonna hurt somebody. There was no way out of it.

"Carlos...I don't love you the way you love me. I'm sorry," I said.

"You're sorry? Are you fucking serious? Then what the fuck were we doing for the past month?" he said.

"We were having a good time. I thought that's what you wanted too. I mean, you're ten years older than me—"

He interrupted me

"So this is about age? So fucking what—that's something we can't change but we're still grown."

"I'm eighteen, Carlos. Look, it doesn't matter. The point is I can't be your girl. I can't have too much going on. I have to focus on this college shit."

"You don't think I know that? I love that you do that shit. I'm proud of you. I won't get in the way of that."

he said. He moved next to me and put his arms around me, his mouth on my neck.

"I just can't, okay?"

I could feel tears coming and it wasn't cool. I couldn't cry, not right now. Carlos moved away from me.

"I see. So what we just did right now—that was just for show? To piss off JB or something?" he asked.

Fuck. My stomach was killing me. I was a complete asshole. I didn't answer him. Just kept staring down at my cigarette almost gone.

"You know, the fucking joke's on me isn't it? I can't believe I thought you were…special. You totally fucking played me," he said.

"Oh, I played you? I'm not the one hiding two kids and still fucking my kids' mom behind my back," I said defensively.

He looked dead at me. It was like I just kicked him in the gut. He stared into me with those soft, brown eyes and it was then I knew this would be the last time I would ever see him.

"You know guerita, you never stuck around long enough after I fucked you for me to even tell you what's up. And just so we're fucking clear, I'm not fucking my kids' mom."

He got up, buttoned his pants, and then placed a small box on my bed.

"Like I said, I thought you were special."

Then he left. I was alone in the dark apartment on Mission Street. I let the tears come because at that point I had no choice. It wasn't like my other mistakes. Those times, I was the one who got hurt. And at this point in life I was so used to it that it was almost comforting.

It was so familiar that I took it for normal. But this, I had no excuse. I opened the box Carlos left on my bed. It was a gold necklace with "Missy" as a name-plate in little diamonds. I had told Carlos how I always wanted a necklace like this growing-up but my dad wouldn't let me or my sister Espi wear shit like that. The necklace and big hoop earrings weren't allowed, because my dad thought that made us look like cholas and he kept saying that God only gave him good girls. In fact, when Espi got pregnant again, my dad blamed her big hoop earrings before anything else. But the necklace. I had told Carlos that I was gonna try to save my money and buy it for myself because I never do shit like that. Looks like he beat me to it.

It started to rain and the drops were loud against the window pane. I put the necklace away, got under the covers, closed my eyes and wished to be anywhere else.

FOUR-LETTER WORDS

It was time to face the facts: I had only been in the Bay Area a total of three months and I had managed to make and lose one friend in one town, make a lover out of a friend in another, lose them too, and start burning bridges in both. It was October, getting colder. I wasn't use to wearing a jacket all the time, staying in-doors. Trapped. And the arrests at the Vets Hall for under-age drinking made the punk shows fade into the gray skies and empty beaches.

I was going to drop-out of college. I was over it. Really over it.

I called JB and told him the good news.

"Wow, you are so fucking stupid," was all he said.

"Excuse me?"

"You heard me—you are really blowin' it, dude."

"It's not like you went to college. Look at all the adventures you've had—"

"And shit jobs, and shit apartments, and even shittier missed opportunities."

I started to cry. It was becoming an all too common bad habit of mine.

"Look, you're young. Real young. And that's... awesome. Seriously, that's so fucking awesome. Don't grow-up too fast, Missy. At least stay 'til the end of the year. After that, you have my complete blessing to make all the mistakes your sweet heart desires."

Okay. Fine. End of the year. I could do that.

A week later I met a girl named Christina who played guitar and smoked generic cigarettes. She was the first person I met at school that actually stuck, and she was like me—Mexican and from LA, and we shared records and a lot of stupid jokes. In fact, she had been living right down the hall from me in my dorm the whole time, though I never remembered seeing her. The last few months were a definite blur. I hardly slept in the bed the school gave me. I'd been going back and forth between Santa Cruz and San Francisco so much that I never knew what day it was and sometimes, I'd walk for hours, thinking I was going to my favorite record store or thrift store in one town only to realize that the reason I couldn't find it was because I was in the other town. And the park. The old squat. I would somehow find myself back there again, thinking that I was going to see Anarchy. Only to arrive and see it empty. Then the memory would come back that she split, way split, and then I'd sit under the bridge for a minute before I figured out what to do next. College. The scholarship. JB's words. They were the only things really holding me down right now. I wasn't a quitter, either. I had my "good-girl" act down, so hard, that it gnawed at my ego to just up and walk away. That shit was for Anarchy. And Carlos. Fuck man—Carlos couldn't even stick around for his own kids, his flesh and blood. Why the fuck would he stick around for me? And why would he stick around for me. He was my dirty secret. So fucking annoying, feelings. Why couldn't things just ever be easy, chill? Everything had to be mapped out, scheduled, planned. Every place had a routine, a scene. I started to realize I couldn't keep up with it all. But I was finally making serious cash at Harry's. And my grades were pretty good, considering I didn't really get "grades". At least up here, I had what I wanted all along—freedom. I just came and went. No one waiting around for me, not like that happened too much before anyways. For the first time, I really didn't belong anywhere. I was boundless, unchartered. It hit me, right then—sitting in the park under the same tree where Anarchy would find me two months ago, just how good I had it. I decided to give the beach-town a second chance.

Christina told me about a house show downtown. House shows were all I had known in LA—groups of punks, or squatters who managed to have a house to themselves where they threw punk shows in the living room, usually for about thirty minutes since that's how long it took before the cops came and broke it all up. I'd never been to one in Santa Cruz, but Christina insisted we go because there would be "people like 'us' there." I didn't know what the fuck she was talking about but that proved to be the case most of the time, so I just kept my mouth shut and away we went.

It was almost November, still jacket-weather. I broke-down and bought a dark blue bomber jacket from a thrift store in the Haight since I threw-away Carlos'. Fuck him. Fuck his lies. Fuck him calling me a liar. Fuck all the ways he knew how to fuck, and it was good, and deep down I missed him so much all I could think about was fucking a million other vatos, hoping I could just fuck him out of me. And fuck not getting fucked for over a month now. Yeah. Fuck that, too.

Christina and I successfully got lost within five minutes. I hadn't spent much time in that area of town. I knew the name of the street, Escalona. But knowing names is different than knowing places and I was ready to quit after only a few unfamiliar blocks of houses, hills, watching my breath become mist on the exhale. That is, until we heard the warm sound of drums and four cords only five houses ahead.

"See, all isn't lost yet!" she said.

Her positive attitude was refreshing. Anarchy and I would have given up after one block, sat down on the curb together, and started snorting or drinking something. But Christina was one of those straight-edge girls. The worst thing she did was smoke those nasty, generic cigarettes of hers and she was even working on quitting that. I had to admit, it was nice having a conversation that didn't involve scoring or how to execute the next big hustle. I actually felt normal around her, which made me trust her, which made me somewhat bearable to be around.

We walked closer to the house, and it was definitely the spot. There were lots of punks but not just any punks…girls. Lots of girl-punks. In fact, there were maybe about five visible dudes in a sea of punk-chicks.

"Are those really all girls?" I asked.

Christina laughed.

"Um, yes. What, you've never been to a Riot Grrrl show before?"

"A riot what?"

"Riot Grrrl. You know, girl punk bands."

"As in, all the bands are girls?"

"Yes! All the bands are girls! I mean, some have one guy in them, maybe two. But they're all girl bands."

"So, what do they talk about?"

Christina kept looking at me like I was the dumbest motherfucker on the block.

"You've really never heard of Riot Grrrl? It's 1996 and you've really never heard of it?"

"Well, I've heard of it. But don't those girls live in Olympia or something? And aren't they all…you know…gay?"

"They're not all gay! But I'm sure a lot of them are. I mean, aren't you…"

"Gay? Well…I guess. But I fuck dudes too, you know? And I don't know any gays. I mean, not up here," I said.

"Well, I'm like you and we know each other. If I'm half-gay and you're half-gay then together we are one full-gay so now we can say we know gays. Look, is it gonna be a problem?" she said.

"No! Fuck no it's not a problem! I'm not fucked-up like that!" I said defensively.

"Good, let's go inside then." She smiled.

I was confronted by throngs of faces I'd never seen before, all female. All staring me up and down. Christina seemed so relaxed, so I tried to follow her lead. It occurred to me as much as I was attracted to them, I wasn't used to being around girls unless I was dancing naked in a room with neon lights and a pole against my back. The looks were similar, all checking me out, all trying to make something out of me, see what I was. I decided that's how all groups of chicks were. Which was exactly why I steered clear of them unless I was getting paid. And I wasn't getting paid to be here, with all of them. So I really didn't understand what the hell I was doing there. But in a world where you got nothing—nothing to do, nothing to look forward to, nothing to attach to—why the fuck not?

We made it into the house, past the first round of stares, into the living room where there was a band playing. It was the second band, which shocked me because in LA the house shows almost never made it to the second band before they were shut-down. We stood in the back, watching for a little while. It was different, being present at a show. I mean, I hadn't even had a drink yet. I saw people holding drinks and it gave me comfort to know that it was an option, especially since I had no idea how to be in this place. I tried standing about five different ways before Christina suggested that I take off my jacket and stand against the wall for a minute.

I kept scanning the party to see if there was anyone, just one person, I knew. Even someone I didn't really know, but saw at a show before. No one. Not a single person looked familiar.

"I'm gonna go outside and smoke. You okay by yourself?" Christina said.

"Yeah, yeah I'm okay," I said, acting cool.

But I wasn't cool. Being there I knew it. It was the first time I even cared about being cool. One thing was for sure, I was used to being alone. That, I knew how to do real good.

The band finished. Girls were milling about, some going outside, some turning to each other to talk or just make-out. I was a total fucking alien. I didn't even know any of the bands these girls had stitched onto their vests and jackets. Bikini Kill. Heavens to Betsy. Bratmobile. I felt like they were a part of some great big secret scene.

"Dead Kennedys? Aren't they, like, a bunch of sexist white dudes who drink too much beer?" some girl said, pointing to my jacket.

"Yeah, gross huh? It came with the jacket, I just haven't had time to take it off," I said, pushing the jacket behind me so no one else could read the names of the other bands that I'm sure were equally disgusting to this crowd: Black Flag, The Misfits.

I just kept standing and waiting for Christina to come back so I could just get the fuck out of there. It was not my scene. I didn't know this punk world. It was high school all over again. Not knowing the right things to say, not having the right bands on my jacket, not knowing anyone. It was stupid and fake and not for me. I didn't care if these were all punk-chicks, I didn't care if they were all fucking each other—*I need to get the hell out of here, now,* I thought. I decided not to try and head to the back of the house to find Christina, since there were just more faces, more staring. I just had to leave. I was heading to the door when a hand grabbed me.

"Hey—Los Crudos. That's a really good band. I've never even met another person whose ever heard of them. Well, unless they spoke Spanish," said the voice.

I looked up, and there was this person. I say person, because I couldn't tell whether they were a girl or a boy. But it was the first kind words I'd gotten since I walked through the door, so it sure as shit didn't matter.

"What?"

"Your jacket, you have a Los Crudos patch on it. That's for the band, right?" the voice continued.

"Yeah, yeah it is," I said.

"I love that song, "Levantate"? That's one of my favorite songs," the voice said.

"Me too—I have a live version of it from a house show in Mexico City last year," I said excitedly, like a stupid fifteen-year-old.

"Wow—that's really cool. I'm Tommy."

Tommy extended a hand towards me and I took it.

"I'm Missy. Missy Fuego."

"Wow, is that your real name?" Tommy smiled.

"Yes, it's actually my real name. It's my first and middle name. My dad named me. It's a long story. My last name is actually Gonzalez." I smiled back, a little shy, my guard still up not sure if I was being teased.

"Mine is Moreno. It means 'Brown' which is kind of a joke I guess since I look more olive," Tommy laughed.

"Well, I look guerita, but I'm Mexican too. I came to this country when I was four."

"Well, I was born in Livermore, in the East Bay which arguably could be its own country."

I laughed. I don't know what happened—it just slipped out.

"You have a good laugh," Tommy said.

"I'm actually on my way out," I replied.

"Oh, really? That's too bad. Are you waiting for your boyfriend or girlfriend…"

"I don't have one of those. I came with a friend but it looks like I've lost her to the backyard," I said.

"You mean my backyard."

"This is your house?"

"Yes. And my band is playing next. Four Letter Words?"

"The name of your band is Four Letter Words?"

"Yeah, I know, it's kind of a stupid name." Tommy smiled.

"No, no. It's…different."

I kept standing, talking. Tommy was wearing Dickies, a dirty white t-shirt, and a hat that had the word 'Fag' written across it. I could feel something happening and it was bad, real bad. It was the same feeling I had for Anarchy and definitely the same feeling I had for Carlos. Those feelings led to trouble, nothing but trouble. I wanted to escape but my mouth kept talking and laughing and doing that smiling thing and I could feel my face get a little hot. I agreed to stay. Even after Tommy's band played, I stayed longer and we kept talking about politics and college and shit I never talked about at shows mostly because I was fucked up. Before I knew it I stayed past 3am.

"You can stay, if you want. My room is down that hallway…" Tommy said.

"No. I mean, no thank you," I said quickly.

"Well at least let me walk you home…"

"No, no thank you," I said even quicker. Carlos was good boot-camp. I knew, now, how love operated. It started with talking, then laughing, then walking me home. It was all down-hill from there. It only turned into fucking, then lying, then fighting, then nothing. It was best to nip this shit in the bud now, right now.

"I had a good time. Thanks. Maybe I'll see you around."

"I would really like that, Missy Fuego."

I stepped outside and almost fell down the front steps of the house. I realized I had tripped over someone. It was Christina.

"Tina?"

"Yes, that is me."

"Are you drunk?"

"Yes. Yes I am. Is that you, Missy?"

"Yeah, it's me. What happened?"

"You know, I've been sitting on these stairs for the last two hours asking…myself…the same question…"

I lifted her to her feet. This was a dance I knew how to be the lead to. I threw one of her arms over my shoulder, held her up with my other arm, and we walked back to school. Back to the beds with our names on the door, the moon full and clear over our heads.

BOI DYKES AND PEEP SHOWS

I woke-up the next morning on the floor of Christina's room and even though I didn't have a single drink the night before, I couldn't remember how the fuck I ended up there. And then a face peered down on me.

"Hello."

It was a young Chicana. She smiled so easily at me. I flinched a little bit.

"Sorry, I didn't mean to scare you," she said.

"You didn't. I just didn't expect anyone else to be here," I said.

"I'm Gabriella, Christina's roommate."

"Oh, hi. I'm Missy, from down the hall," I said, relieved. I started to get up.

"I know, Christina told me all about you. I don't mean to sound rude, but I've never met a girl with a shaved-head before. Especially a Mexican," she said, still smiling.

I managed to get up to my feet and realized I had no pants on.

"Your pants are over there, on the desk chair." Gabriella pointed.

"Thank you," I said, embarrassed.

"Sure."

Gabriella went over to her bed and began putting freshly folded clothes into her dresser.

"Do you know what time it is?"

"It's two in the afternoon," she replied.

"Fuck, are you serious?"

"Afraid so. Did you miss class or something?"

"No, I just have to get to the city, I have to work tonight," I said.

"Oh wow—you work in the city? That sounds exciting."

I put my pants on and could see Christina in her bed, or rather a huge lump of a human encased in blankets.

"What do you do?"

"What?" I said.

"In the city—where do you work?"

"I…"

I hadn't told anyone in Santa Cruz that I danced, except for Anarchy. It was the first time I was confronted with this question and already I was procrastinating, looking fucking guilty.

"I work in a club," I stammered.

"Wow! And you're eighteen? Do you have a fake I.D.?"

"What?"

"I'm sorry. My mother says I would make more friends if I wasn't so nosy," Gabriella said, looking down.

"You're not nosy," I said.

Her sweetness and shyness were cute. I looked cute but I was never sweet. My full name is Melissa. My abuelita named me. It's supposed to mean "honey-bee; one who brings sweetness". Best intentions, I guess.

"Anyways—what time do you have to be at work?"

"Well I keep late-ass hours. I mean, late hours." She was so sweet that I felt bad for cussing, like I was corrupting her from the start.

"I should be fine," I reassured her.

"Well, you don't have to stay and talk with me if you have to get going. I mean, Christina will be fine. It's not the first time she's done this, she'll wake-up by dinner. Shoot—I didn't mean she's a drunk or anything. I'm not judging. I'm just saying..." she kept fucking around with the clothes and looking down.

"I just meant you can go if you have to. I'll tell her you had to leave and go to work," Gabriella said, quickly returning to her clean laundry.

"Yeah, the bus ride can sometimes be three hours with traffic and I have to do some stuff before work—"

"I could give you a ride? If you want. I have a car..."

"I..." Shit. Shit shit shit shit.

"I'm sorry. I just met you. I'm sure you can't bring people to your work or whatever. My mother says if I wasn't so pushy I would be able to meet more people..."

"You're not pushy. Thank you—but I'm okay taking the bus and I still have time. Thank you. Maybe we can talk again sometime."

"Yeah! I mean, yeah, yeah that would be cool," she beamed.

"And thanks for telling Christina I had to go. I'll call her tomorrow, probably."

"Sure, sure."

I collected my pants and went back down the hall to my room to get my weekend bag ready: high-high-heels, thong that completely covered my pussy (a strict rule at Harry's, believe it or not), bikini tops, black bob wig, make-up bag. I thought about leaving this shit at JB's but I was so paranoid about somebody finding it, like one of his bandmates or that it would get jacked. As much as you're not supposed to have on, the stuff you do wear in the club is more expensive than anyone knows—one pair of shoes alone for work is almost two-hundred dollars for me. I guess you could call it an investment.

I caught my usual Greyhound to the city, rolled in about 7pm, jammed over to my house at JB's to do my usual waiting or nap-time before I got to the club about nine. I had been working the night shift the last month and I was lucky. There was talk of San Francisco cracking-down on North Beach, meaning they were fed-up with what everyone knows to be "Stripper Row". Harry's was situated in the heart of Stripper Row, a literal block and a half of nothing but strip clubs, peep shows, and a few erotic boutiques which is a nice name for sex shop. These "boutiques" also had back rooms with private porn theaters and even some peep shows though everyone knew that if you wanted to see a peep show, you went to Stilettos. I heard a rumor that all the dancers there were lez and after months of working right across the street I still couldn't find the courage to just walk my ass in there. I had to admit, I didn't get why any girl would work a peep show. Every girl knew the worst money was in peep shows. Imagine standing in the doorway of a tiny room, all day, I'm talking hours—waiting for some dude to roll through and, hopefully, choose your tiny room to get a show in. I did the math once—they sometimes don't even make ten bucks an hour. A girl could make that just waiting tables or working in a fucking bar, clothes on, no creeps in sight. Well, mostly.

I was definitely in this for the money and dancing on a pole, giving lap dances that made me at least two-hundred on a slow night or a day shift which I decided was worth my time since the bus was ten dollars round-trip from school to the city then back again. I paid my rent at JB's in one night and the rest of my money was mine, all mine. Even with my scholarship school was costing me up the ass. Plus, it was easy. I mean, too easy. Show-up on-time, get naked for a few hours, go home with a wad of cash. Do this two nights in a row. School during the week. Keep my mouth shut about the whole thing. Then, repeat.

I was actually making real friends at school and in Santa Cruz, I was getting nervous about people finding out what I did for money. Okay, I was worried about my new gay life finding out about what I did for money. All the dykes in Santa Cruz seemed to be into Riot Grrrl and feminism and women getting respect and all that. Those chicks were always talking about how "degrading" porn was and that stripping was just like prostitution and ruined lives. I wanted them to like me. I needed them to like me. The thought of being rejected again was all too familiar, it haunted me. I couldn't let it happen. I had to keep things under-wraps for as long as possible no matter what. This meant more lying, more half-truths. Fuck.

I worked my shift as usual. It was 3 am by the time I was changed into my usual punk-non-descript uniform of Dickies, baby-tee, Vans, shaved head, a little lipstick, fitted bomber jacket. I stepped onto the street, ready to walk to Market and hail a cab when a voice rang out to me in the early morning darkness.

"Missy? Hey!"

Oh. My. Fucking. God. It was Tommy. It was fucking Tommy from Santa Cruz yelling my name, my real name, on Stripper Row at three in the morning. She ran up to me, excited to see me.

"Hey! I thought that was you! What are you doing here? Meeting someone too?" Tommy said.

"Um…"

I was taken totally off-guard. It was late and I had just gotten off work and the shock of seeing her must have been written all over my stupid face. I couldn't come up with a fucking lie fast enough.

"Wait—" Tommy said, walking towards the window of Harry's where some of the photos of the dancers were posted. Where my photo was posted.

"Is that—is this you? That's you, isn't it?" she said, pointing to my picture with the name "Roxy" underneath it.

I continued to stand there with my dumb look and I tried to open my mouth but when I did no words would come out. None at all.

"I…"

"That's you. This is why you come to the city every weekend."

There was just no way to talk my way out of this without sounding like a complete dumbass or worse a complete fucking liar. So, I decided to admit defeat. The thought of meeting girls, maybe even falling in love with one, having friends—it was a nice dream, I thought. But not for me I guess. Whatever.

"Yeah, that's me," I said firmly.

"Wow—it almost doesn't even look like you. That's so fucking crazy!" she said.

"So, I guess you think I'm a big Feminist-Lesbo-Traitor or something and you never wanna speak to me again. Fine. Cool."

I started to walk down the street when Tommy grabbed my arm and stopped me.

"What are you talking about? I don't care. Seriously Missy, I don't fucking care."

She smiled at me after saying this and it occurred to me that maybe, just maybe, I had made my first real friend in the tiny beach-town.

"Really? Because I haven't told anyone in Santa Cruz except for this one chick but she doesn't live there anymore, she moved to Seattle I think. So, nobody then—" I was rambling off words faster than I could put the sentences together. There was a huge relief in just telling someone the truth about me and actually having them not care that I couldn't stop talking. Until Tommy interrupted me.

"Seriously, it's cool! It's totally cool with me. And I'll keep my mouth shut about it. I promise," she said.

I felt my heart leave my throat and go back into my chest. I couldn't fucking believe it. Maybe there really was a God. Or Goddess. Or both. Whatever, what-fucking-ever I didn't care. This was the chance, the gift I was waiting for. And I wasn't gonna fuck it up. Not this time.

"Wait, what the fuck are you doing here? At three in the morning? What the fuck are you even doing in the city?" I asked.

"You're not the only one with secrets. C'mon, I gotta go back across the street," Tommy said with a smile.

We walked back and stood out front of Stilettos, the twenty-four-hour peep show on Stripper Row. After a few minutes I saw another familiar face.

"Hey Missy. And hey you," she said to Tommy as they started kissing. It was this other boi-dyke, Gretchen, from Santa Cruz. She went by the nickname "Gretch." She was into punk too and she worked at the Feminist bookstore in-town called Our Space.

"What are you doing here?" I asked Gretch.

She pointed to the front-door of Stilettos.

"I work here on Friday and Saturday nights for the next two months. I'm covering for a friend. What are you doing here?"

"I work at Harry's, across the street," I replied.

"Ooooh I've always wanted to go in there but I work in the booth every time I'm here and can't get away. I love pole-dancing! You must make good money there," she said excitedly.

"I do alright."

"Well, now that we all know each other better than expected, you wanna join us, Missy?" Tommy chimed in.

"Oh yeah! Come with us! We're going to Smashed," Gretch said.

"What's Smashed?" I asked suspiciously.

"Trust me, you'll like it," Tommy said.

We got into Tommy's Toyota corolla and drove into the belly of the city.

A TALE OF TWO ONE-NIGHT STANDS

We drove deep into the SOMA district which is mostly warehouses and half-empty buildings. I'd heard a lot of raves happened in this area because the building owners were desperate to get any kind of money out of the space. We parked in front of a thin doorway with dark, neon lights pouring out of it and a dude leaning against the frame with a six-inch Mohawk.

"Password, ladies," he said in a friendly, feminine voice.

"I love trash," Tommy said with a grin.

And just like that, we each paid two bucks and walked through the door.

I'd been to a couple gay bars when I first landed in San Francisco but no real clubs. There wasn't even a bar just for women, only women's nights at gay bars in the Castro. There was one club I'd heard of for chicks but it was only once a month and I could never go because I danced at Harry's Friday nights. And, those places weren't my scene. It was mostly digitized dance music and most of the women were much older than me and seemed only interested in each other. I'd just about given up on San Francisco as a place for me to meet girls since I was only there three days a week, mostly working, and mostly around straight punks, which really meant straight white boys who acted thirteen-years-old.

"Let's walk around!" Tommy shouted in my ear over the loud music.

It wasn't just any music either. It was punk and rock n' roll. Already a nice change of pace.

We walked around the open space of a fairly small warehouse. It was dark and dirty. There were wooden crates to sit on and a few old-looking couches where people were making-out. Then there was a part that was sectioned off by some sheets to look like its own room.

"What's that?" I asked Tommy.

Tommy laughed.

"That's a hook-up room."

"A what?" I said.

"A hook-up room. People go in there just to hook-up, to have sex."

*Okay...*I thought. At the sake of sounding like a fucking school-girl, what the fuck had I gotten myself into?

"Oh," I said.

We found a spot to sit and Gretch went to what was considered the "bar"—a long table with two kegs of beer behind it, some sodas on the table, some mixers, vodka, and what looked like other hard liquor next to them with another mohawked boy standing guard—to get us some drinks. It was then that I was able to take this place in: it was a gay punk club. Boys and girls. What were the odds?

I felt incredibly self-conscious. I decided right then and there that I just wasn't cool enough to be there. Tommy seemed so relaxed, like this was her element. She was smiling and leaning back as she sat. I sat straight-up, good-ass posture and all. I even kept my jacket on.

"Dude, take your jacket off," Tommy said.

"No, I'm okay."

"Seriously, take your jacket off. I promise you won't regret it."

I did what I was told. Gretch came back with the drinks. I hoped it was just beer but it wasn't.

"What is this?" I asked her.

"It's my special creation. I call it 'a tale of two one-night stands'. You know, like the Amistad Maupin book 'A Tale of Two Cities'? This is definite fuck juice," Gretch said with a proud grin.

"Fuck juice?" I repeated.

"Yes. Drink this and you will want to fuck and get fucked. This drink has a ninety-eight percent guarantee," she shouted over Tribe 8 blaring out of the speakers.

"What's in it?" I asked.

"Just drink it! Not knowing is half the fun!" Gretch shouted enthusiastically.

I looked at Tommy for reassurance. She was already drinking out of her cup so I figured what could it hurt, and did the same. It tasted very sweet and the warehouse had no ventilation so I drank it faster than you could say "fuck juice."

Gretch and Tommy started making out inches away from me and realizing that three's-a-crowd I got up and decided to walk around by myself. But the more steps I took the more I just wanted to sit down, and not just anywhere but somewhere comfortable. Gretch wasn't fucking playing—that drink was going straight to my head. A lot of the couches were taken and I considered just sitting on the damn floor until I peeked inside the hook-up room.

No one was in there. I walked in and helped myself to one of the couches, completely spreading out on it. I could feel my head moving to the sound of the music coming out of the shitty speakers. My brain was doing its own slam-dancing, pulsing with each vibration and speck of re-verb. It didn't hurt, but I could feel my body's effort and that made me a little anxious so I closed my eyes and decided to concentrate. Like most drunks, I thought if I just stopped moving or got as low to the ground as possible I could regain control. This always happened to me drinking, which is why it was no surprise I would be found on the ground all over Santa Cruz and San Francisco. Concrete was my favorite. It felt solid, flat, an even fortress and my small frame would sink into it like a water-bed. I decided it was time for the floor. But as I slowly rose off the couch, getting ready to make my move, a girl with pink hair and really nice tits stood in front of me.

"Hi," she said.

"Hi," I mumbled and waved. I waved because I couldn't hear myself talk and I wanted to make sure she understood me.

"I know we just met, but would you mind putting this glove on your hand and sticking it inside me?"

I wasn't sure if she really said what she just said so I said to her what seems to come out of my mouth a lot lately.

"What?"

"Now? Now, please. Will you please just put this glove on and stick your hand inside of me now? I'm so close it's crazy…" she said.

Then she handed me the glove, got next to me on the couch, lifted the tiniest skirt I'd ever seen on a girl, spread her legs open, no underwear just straight-up pussy hangin' out, started rubbing those awesome tits of hers under her tiny-tee-shirt, and waited for me. I admit, I did look around for a moment. We were the only two in there from what I could see.

"Please, I'm so ready…" she moaned.

So, I did it. I put the glove on my right hand, gently slipped two fingers inside her, and began to work.

"Oooohhh, you can put more in there…" she moaned again.

So I did. I first slid one more, then a moment later another, all the while her grinding on-top of my hand faster and faster.

"Yes! Yes, yessssss…" she moaned.

It was then that I looked down at my hand, my "fucking-hand" and realized my entire hand was inside of her, working away. She got louder and louder to the point where she was practically screaming over the music and let me tell you that was not easy to do. That fucking music was fucking loud as fuck.

"Yes! Yes! Fuck, yes! Here it comes!"

And like that, she came, everywhere. All over my hand, all over the thrift-store couch. Just clear liquid gushing out of her like a broken faucet.

"Rip your hand out of me!" she screamed.

I did. Hard. Fast. Instinct, really. Her juices dripped down my gloved hand toward my elbow. I saw a roll of paper towels next to the couch which was very convenient, I thought. I cleaned my arms up, took the glove off and wrapped it in the used paper towel. The pink-haired girl pushed her skirt down, got up, turned to me and said "Thank You."

She stood upright and walked out of the hook-up room. It occurred to me that this was the first time I was actually somebody's sex-toy. Gretch's fuck-juice was running through me so fast that it didn't even occur to me to be offended or feel used. Instead I felt very useful. Almost like I was doing a community service. My hands were small, nothing to write home about, but there was this hot chick who needed them and that was pretty alright.

I stumbled out of the hook-up room and found a trashcan, throwing away the evidence. I planned to walk towards Tommy and Gretch but as I approached I could see Tommy fucking Gretch with a strap-on right out in the open area of the club so I turned around and decided to find a bathroom, then some floor to spread out on. On my way to the bathroom I saw another girl, about my height and weight, very ordinary looking. She didn't have any part of her head shaved like so many of us there. She wore black-rimmed glasses, had brown hair with ordinary bangs that hung softly against her forehead. She was wearing black pants and a black t-shirt. I probably would have missed her in any other setting but here— here she stood out.

"That was pretty spectacular," the girl with the glasses said with a smile.

"What was?" I asked.

"Back there. That was pretty cool to watch." She pointed to the hook-up room.

I was confused. I was sure that I didn't see anyone else in there.

"I was peeking at you two from in between the curtains outside of the room," she clarified.

"Oh," I said.

"I'm sorry, I didn't mean to make you feel weird. This is your first time here isn't it?"

"I guess it's written all over my face," I tried to joke out of embarrassment.

"It's okay. I just haven't seen you here before and I think I would remember you," she said smiling.

"I'm Missy," I said, hand outstretched.

"Wow, the infamous hand. I'm Jane," the girl said.

We shook hands. Of course she was Jane. *Plain Jane,* I thought. I'd never met an actual girl with that name.

"Your name is really Jane?" I asked.

"Yeah, the most ordinary name in the world does actually get chosen sometimes," she said.

She smiled again. I liked her smile. It seemed honest.

"Are you heading to the bathroom?" she said.

"Yes."

"Mind if I follow you?"

She walked behind me into the bathroom where I pissed in the toilet and then hovered over it a little thinking I might throw-up, but amazingly it was a false-alarm. I felt great actually. Drunk, definitely drunk. But good. Jane was standing against the wall. It was the kind of bathroom with only one toilet and the door manually locked behind you.

"Look I know we just met and all and I know you just had a good-time back there. But I saw you the second you walked through the door and if it's cool with you, I'd like to make-out with you in this bathroom. Right now," she said.

She walked towards me. I wore glasses too and took them off because it was clear Jane was moving in before I could fully respond. But she just stood there, in front of me, with one hand at my waist and the other touching my face.

"Your move," she whispered in my ear.

I took it. I put my hands on her hips and kissed her. I'd never kissed anyone my own height before and I liked it, it was so easy to find her face. And the kiss was hot, very hot. We kept kissing, just kissing, and I pulled her against me, where we both landed against the wall and kept kissing. It was so nice. I have no idea how long we were making-out in there, but it must've been awhile because I had no more lipstick on—it was all over her mouth. Jane wasn't wearing any so she looked like she'd been drinking red kool-aid, the redness a soft stain against her mouth. I was lost in her. Then the door swung open.

"I knew it! I found her Gretch!" Tommy yelled behind her.

I pulled away a little, feeling caught. Jane just kept kissing my neck and pulled me back to her.

"How's it going?" I said to Tommy.

Tommy laughed.

"I'll give you five minutes then meet us outside, 'kay? They're closing."

I turned back to kissing Jane. Just a little more, why not?

"I guess it's time to go," I said.

"Yeah," she said.

"So can I call you?"

"I'm sure we'll see each other again soon," Jane said.

She then smiled and walked out of the bathroom. I cleaned up a little in the dirty sink, then walked out to meet Tommy.

The three of us stepped onto the street and it was starting to become light outside. It was five in the morning, and we decided to head to the Castro for twenty-four-hour breakfast.

"So, 'fuck-juice' worked out for you?" Gretch said smiling.

"Yes."

"So…" Tommy said.

"So…I had one anonymous and one semi-anonymous," I said.

"What? You hooked-up twice? With two different girls?" Tommy said.

"Yes."

"It's always the first-timers. I swear I need to copyright that drink or patent it or something," Gretch said.

"What was the other one?" Tommy said.

"I stuck my hand inside a pink-haired girl in the hook-up room."

"How many fingers?" Gretch asked.

"All of them," I said in-between bites of my scrambled eggs.

"Holy fucking shit! Your first time out and you fisted a girl at Smashed! I fucking swear! I was never that lucky! It took me several times of going to that club before anything happened to me!" Tommy said.

"I guess I'm a natural."

I smeared my toast in my eggs.

THE F-WORD

I started hanging out with Tommy a lot. Besides playing guitar in Four Letter Words she also went to the college. She was a couple years ahead of me. She was a boi-dyke, always in the same baseball cap, Dickie's, combat boots, an array of cool t-shirts she neatly hung up on thick, plastic hangers in her closet. Sometimes she ironed them and it was details like this that reminded me of my older brother ironing the crease down his chinos and Ben Davis early in the morning, the smell of the street in my old neighborhood— home.

She was vegetarian, I'd never met a Chicano who didn't eat meat. She spent hours with me talking about books, bands, ideas, politics all while getting drunk on cheap wine at the beach, another Santa Cruz sunset behind us. And she was a feminist. A Xicana Feminist.

"Whoa," I said.

"What? You're acting like I have a disease or something," Tommy laughed.

"So, you don't eat meat, you're gay, and you hate men—"

"Stop stop stop stop, time out, wait a minute, I never said I hate men. Is that really what you think?" She interrupted me.

I looked down, embarrassed. Fuck. I couldn't afford to lose another potential friend. I figured the truth might fuck me, but lying to Tommy? That was a risk I couldn't afford to take.

"I'm…I mean, I guess I honestly don't know what I mean…" I stammered.

Tommy took a sip of Mexican coke.

"It's okay—just don't assume, okay?"

Rule #1. Don't assume. Noted.

"You know I just got hired at the feminist bookstore downtown…"

I'd passed by that place many times, there were always a lot of really hot girls there with tattoos and piercings—but I didn't have the courage to go inside. Now Tommy was gonna be working there. I bet all those girls are feminists too. I began to feel a little anxious that maybe I wasn't cool enough for Tommy.

"When were you gonna tell me you got the job?"

"I'm telling you now. Why do you sound worried?" Tommy laughed and punched me in the arm.

"I don't know…"

"You'll like it there," Tommy said.

The day I had been dreading finally came, when Tommy asked me to meet her at Our Space and hangout with her during her shift. I realized Riot Grrrls were one thing, but full on feminists? And were there other Xicana Feminists besides Tommy in Santa Cruz? And what did you have to do to get into that clique? It was more rules, more paying attention, more notes. I wasn't sure I could keep up with all this new-ness.

"I don't think I can make it. I have school crap…" I lied when Tommy phoned to remind me.

"Oh fucking c'mon! You can do that later! Gretch works there too now, she closes the café every Thursday night. Just…c'mooooooooon!" she started whining into the phone.

"Okay okay okay okay okay okay I'll be there, I gotta go."

I hung up and started figuring out what to wear—do feminists even care about that stuff? I just remember the house show at Tommy's, the Riot Grrrls making fun of my patches, the bands I liked— I really wasn't up for that bullshit again. I decided on a Tribe 8 t-shirt, my cleanest pair of dark blue Dickie's, my docs, and the most innocent, non-make-up-looking lip color I could find in case there were make-up triggers. I didn't even know if it was true, but my mother always told me that first impressions are everything, absolutely everything.

My mom. I hadn't really thought about her since I'd left LA. She still wasn't speaking to me, but that was okay because I wasn't speaking to her either. It had been six months. She came home early from work, and found me and NaTanya making-out in my bedroom. My mother stared at me, then her, then me again. Her face changed as she realized I wasn't who she thought I was. She just stopped talking to me. Then NaTanya broke-up with me because she couldn't handle me working at the club and then the thought of me still doing that up North, miles upon miles away—she'd had enough. I left right after, no real good-bye and not a word since. I wanted so much to never be like her, but here I was right in this moment, putting together an outfit and all the right touches just like my mother. Exactly like my mother.

I decided not to think about her anymore. I didn't need this distraction right now, especially now, when I was finally making things happen my own way. But really, I missed her. And I hated that.

I took the bus downtown, walked the ten minutes from the Metro station over to the tiny side street right off the main drag of Pacific Avenue to Our Space. I was turning the corner, my stomach started to feel real sick and I could feel my body tighten up. I was gonna finally go into Our Space! I was excited but nervous. I felt like every moment, for awhile, would be a test. A test to see if I really fit. I'd been spending so much time in the city—meeting Tommy made me see that maybe I hadn't given Santa Cruz a real chance. I mean, Anarchy and all that stuff that was just one moment, and it was right in the beginning so it couldn't be all there was, right? Plus, my hours at work were already being cut slowly due to crackdowns of Stripper Row. JB and I had made-up over Carlos and were cool but his band was busy, he'd been gone for about a month. I hadn't seen Carlos at all. San Francisco was beautiful in this dirty, fucked up way but for now it was all work, all business, to me. My classes that quarter were more involved, I was basically planted here like one of the many trees that towered around me in the college.

All of these thoughts were pushing to get to the front of my priorities as I walked even closer to the door of Our Space. I decided to stop and smoke a cigarette, maybe give myself a pep talk before I went in, but just as I was fishing the pack out of the front pocket of my jean jacket, a familiar face found me and it was one I didn't expect.

"Hey stranger, where have you been?"

It was Rodney, the bass player in Tommy's band. I'd seen her at the college too, in-between classes. She always seemed to find me.

"Hey, how's it going?" I tried to sound cool, but I was so fucking awkward.

"Are you going to Our Space too?"

"Um…yeah, yeah I'm about to make my way in there." Now I couldn't back out.

I quickly lit up my cigarette as my visual excuse to stay outside. I remember Rodney telling me at school once that she didn't smoke so I thought it might be a good way of getting a little space to myself too. But, she stayed outside and kept talking with me.

"You look nice, are you going somewhere?" she asked.

Once again I felt even more awkward, like I was already overdressed to my first feminist party, another epic fail on my part. But I was there, no turning back.

"Thanks, no it's just laundry day," I lied.

"Well then I'm glad it's laundry day, real glad." Then she smiled, a very sweet smile.

"I should probably get in there, Tommy is expecting me," I said quickly as I put the cigarette out that I'd only lit a few drags ago.

"Look, you should come over sometime, to hang out, listen to records. I know you're just getting into

Riot Grrrl stuff I have a lot of it, I live just down the street from Tommy…"

"Okay, yeah…sure…" I said distracted. I knew I would have to go inside the store and I was panicking a little at the last minute.

"How about next week? Tuesday, 3pm? We can fool around on my bass again too, like we did at Tommy's a couple weeks ago?" she suggested.

"Sure," I replied. Those Riot Grrrls were always like that: try this, try that, let's make plans right now here on the street. Rodney was the first Riot Grrrl that was really nice to me or at least tried to be my friend. She, besides Gretch, was the only white girl I'd willfully spent any time with and she was actually pretty cool.

"See you soon," she said, again with that smile, as she walked past me in her typical Riot Grrrl uniform of vintage dress, torn tights, black flats, jacket with a patch that said 'Grrrls to the front!' on the back.

The moment had come. I took a breath, and walked through the door. Only, there was no one inside. I could hear Bikini Kill loudly playing on the sound-system in the café next door, but no one was in there either. I looked around, it was small but very neat, very organized. There was a porn rental section, lots of postcards and posters of women, the books were divided into sections that were new to me: Xicana Feminism, Black Feminism, Third Wave Feminism, Women's Health, Porn, Third World Consciousness. It looked like a home library or living room inside, with a couple of oversized chairs and a coffee table in the center of the room. The café looked like any other café only all the items were named after goddesses, characters from the show Xena: Warrior Princess, and people, people I assumed were celebrity feminists. I still couldn't find anybody and I almost got worried.

"Tommy! Gretch!" I called out.

Nothing. I called out again as I went back into the bookstore and heard Tommy's voice call back but I couldn't tell from where.

"We're in here!" she said.

"Where?" I yelled.

Then a door swung open from the back of the store. It was Gretch, and she was topless, her right nipple bright pink, almost red, with a huge ring through it.

"We're in here! In the bathroom!"

There was Gretch, Tommy, and another girl I'd never seen before. Tommy and Gretch were topless while the other girl held a needle in her latex-gloved hand and they were laughing.

"Get in here, we're getting our nipples pierced!" Tommy said as she grabbed me by the front of my jacket and pulled me into the Our Space bathroom. They quickly shut the door behind me.

"But the store is still open…"

"Naw, we're technically closed, it's after 9pm," Gretch said.

The third woman outstretched her hand.

"I'm Sheila. You wanna get pierced, sister?"

"Oh, I don't want to interrupt you guys," I said. It was really sinking in that they were both half-naked.

"C'mon dude, just do it. You don't have to get your nipple done. How about, I don't know, your nose? You can have a nose ring, right?" Tommy egged me on.

I didn't really understand what she meant by that. My parents weren't in my life so I was my own boss. But I did work at the club, and they were pretty strict about that kind of thing.

"I'm really good with noses," Sheila said with the needle in her hand.

They were all staring at me, smiling, waiting for my answer.

"Okay, I'll do my nose," I said, taking my seat on top of the toilet.

"Yay!" they all cheered. Being a feminist was turning out to be easier than I thought.

Shelia wiped my nose clean with antibacterial stuff on some toilet paper.

"This is gonna pinch a little, but try to stay still, just yell or something if it's too much," she said.

"Yell or something…"

And before I could finish my thought, Sheila's needle was in my nose.

"Fuck!" I shouted. A little pinch? It felt like a fucking sword going through my face. Sheila pushed a small ring through.

"You have a nose ring. It really suits you, sister, a good choice for you," she said.

They all stood back and looked at my face.

"Seriously, it looks really good on you dude," Tommy said, still shirtless.

I thanked her and blushed.

"And with that, I must go. I gotta get home by ten to nurse the baby." Shelia started packing up her small stash of piercing gear, tied her long dreads behind her, and put on a shawl that fell delicately against her Black skin.

"Don't forget to lock up the back café door sisters, and make sure to clean those new holes with Dial and saline solution at least twice a day for six weeks, I'll see you tomorrow," Sheila said.

Hugs were given all around by her, even to me. Then she left.

"Holy fuck, let's shut this motherfucker down!" Gretch said.

She left the bathroom, still topless, ran into the café and turned the music up a little more, then threw the tiniest tank top over her perfect B-cup tits, the pierced one poking through very proudly. Tommy left next, put her big t-shirt on, same proud nipple hard below the fabric. I was still sitting on the toilet seat trying to figure out what happened. Tommy looked back.

"C'mon and help me in the bookstore."

I got up, helped Tommy sweep, vacuum, dust, while she counted the register. I tidied up the little living room space and started to look at the books on the shelves. I didn't know anything about feminism, especially Xicana Feminism like Tommy, and I was hoping to find a book that would just tell me what to do.

"Hey, I actually got something for you," Tommy said, noticing my browsing.

She handed me a book with the title *Chicana Lesbians: The Girls Our Mothers Warned Us About.*

"I think you'll like this book." Tommy smiled.

"Does it...you know...tell you how to be...you know, a feminist?"

Tommy kept smiling.

"I don't think there's any books like that, but, just read it."

She pushed the book in my hands. Gretch came into the bookstore.

"Café is closed, let's go to your house Tommy."

We locked up the bookstore. I could see my reflection through the glass of the store-front window. The nose ring did look pretty cool on me. Looking at myself I could see the books and part of the café staring back at me and it felt…safe. Really safe. I figured there was something to the F-word, feminism.

RIOT GRRRLS
&
GOLD STARS

I started hanging out at Our Space at least three times a week. The women that went there were different than the ones at the college, but the store got plenty of college girls too. There were Riot Grrrls. I really tried to give those white girls a chance. I decided maybe I was being too judgmental. I'd never really met any white people before and the Riot Grrrls that hung out at Our Space didn't seem like the ones from the house show at Tommy's house. They were the only people close to my age using the F-word plus they were born out of a punk rock movement—I figured I'd get to know them. But after going to a Vegan cooking workshop where myself and all the other Brown and Black girls ended up doing all the cooking and cleaning while the white girls sat and ate the food, told me that I was cool off them. Then I started hanging out with Rodney.

Tommy told me she was a "gold-star" lesbian. I'd never heard that term before and when Tommy explained to me what that meant I was even more skeptical.

"You know, it's a dyke whose never done anything with a dude."

"Fuck you…"

"No, I'm fucking serious."

"Nothing—not even kissing?"

"Nada."

She sounded like a unicorn—a mythical, magical creature that only the true believers can see. Rodney was the bass player in Tommy's band. She was the kid of real hippies. She and her sister grew-up on a hippie commune somewhere in the liberal South. It was called "The Meadow." They didn't have clocks or calendars there and they went to school in some guy's living room and they allowed the kids to do whatever the hell they wanted. They spelled "cat" "k-a-t" and one plus one equals three—shit like that. The "teachers" didn't want to "inhibit" their creativity.

And she had never done a single sexual thing with a boy. She lost her virginity to a girl—and not the "I-had-a-sexual-experience-with-a-girl-like-oral-sex-before-pentration" kind of virginity. But the status quo virginity: she had her hymen broken, by a girl, by choice, during sex.

I immediately secretly hated her and was insanely jealous. What. The. Fuck. It was so fucking unfair. Not to mention she was talented at every aspect of art she took up, especially the bass. I was terrible at instruments. The bass alone was fucking heavy—I couldn't imagine carrying that fuckin' thing everywhere. I was one hundred and ten pounds, really not that strong—I could never get my body in the right position to hold up an instrument like a guitar and I felt like a failure. I just wasn't built for gear and this was another boulder crushing my dream of being in a band. Rodney was small, just like me. She held that thing like she was born with it.

"Come on—just try it," she would say to me. She was really, really nice too which made hating her an extra challenge.

"I just don't think it's for me."

"Oh, don't think like that—so many people want you to think like that. Cuz you're a girl. And the bass is a heavy instrument— when I play chords I actually stay standing..."

Rodney was also a Riot Grrrl—the first one I'd really befriended. She was one of those incredibly supportive Riot Grrrls, not like the racist assholes from the vegan cooking workshop. She just believed you could do anything. So every time I said "no" she would counter with "just try it" and she would fuckin' nag me until I did so I ended up doing all sorts of shit like rock-climbing, changing the oil in Tommy's car, and holding the bass.

"So you've never really done anything with a guy?" I said.

"Oh—yeah. I've played in bands with guys."

"No. I mean you've never gotten down. Sexually. With a penis attached to a man."

"Oh."

She sat down next to me on the bed in her room.

"Well...no."

"Why?"

"I don't know. Because I'm gay."

"Yeah, but. You didn't kiss a boy on the lips when you were little—you know, just to see?"

"No…I mean, I just don't know. I've never really met guys like that." She looked confused.

She didn't seem naïve or childlike. She was simply stating a fact.

"I'm not naïve. I know things like what you're saying happen," she said before I could keep pressing.

"So how did she break your hymen?"

It was too late to be polite—I had to fucking know the secrets of these lezzies if I was ever going to get anywhere in my new gay life. She blushed and laughed a little.

"Well, I was fourteen. And the girl was my first really big crush. She was seventeen."

"Yeah, but did you use something?"

"You mean protection…"

"No! Fuck man—I'm fucking serious! How! How the hell was this accomplished?"

"She used her hand. It took a long time. We waited a couple days to have sex again but when we did, it was amazing. She was able to get her whole hand up there."

"You were fisted too?"

"Yes, what about you?" she laughed.

"What about me…"

My voice trailed off in my annoyingly shy way. The truth was I had never had any of that stuff done to me by a girl. Ever. Oh I had sex with girls—but I was usually the one doing the fucking. I think that's because when I am around girls I'm extremely shy and fucking stupid—I never know when someone likes me unless they just say it to my face. But when I'm lucky enough to get into bed with a girl I immediately go for it and then I feel confident, like I'm good at something. Good at being the fucker. With Anarchy I was on top and I think that surprises the shit out of people because she was more of a tomboy and a dirty punk than me but I don't think that matters. I just wanted to be close to them, all of them.

"So, have you?" Rodney continued.

I was pretty sure she had my number. My secret enemy—the girl I wished I was or at least wanted to be for a day. The girl whose parents encouraged everything she did, even being a big gay and a feminist. And named her a really cool name. I considered lying but what was the point? It wasn't fucking high school—it's not like I hadn't done anything.

"I've had sex. I mean, with girls. A lot. I like girls..."

Fuck. I was sounding very desperate.

"I mean, I haven't had what you had. I did it with a guy and it was over in about fifteen minutes," I said. "Oh—what about a girl?"

I was starting to panic quietly. I was trying to breathe. I kept looking around Rodney's room with the Joan Jett poster on the wall and a million records on the shelves.

"Not done to me, you know. But I don't have any weird hang-ups about it. Like, just because I'm a tomboy or whatever doesn't mean I don't want to. It just never came up."

Rodney moved closer to me. She was the type that held your hand when she talked to you and those people scared the shit out of me. Especially Rodney—she was into the same things as me but very different. She wore skirts, Go-Go boots, make-up. She had incredible skin and shiny, long blonde hair. Her clothes were clean and she smelled like apples. I was in my usual—Vans, dirty Dickie's, a sweatshirt. My head was shaved, my face small but distinct—all parts of me naturally outlined, my lips always resting in a soft pout. I didn't smell bad but all my money went to supplemental tuition payments, life, life, life—I would buy my soap and shampoo at the dollar stores in the city when I'd go to work so I smelled sanitized, almost unnatural. I just couldn't get how someone that looked like her had never been with a single guy in her whole life, and how someone like me just couldn't get dudes to leave me alone.

"Well, you're in Santa Cruz which is kinda Dyke-central. I'm sure you won't have a problem," she said in her supportive-Riot-Grrrl way.

"Why, are you offering?" I said jokingly. More for myself so I wouldn't pass out from embarrassment.

She turned really red and I felt bad because as usual someone was trying to be nice to me and all I knew how to do was be an obnoxious asshole.

"Well, I wouldn't say no…"

Then we sat for a minute. For a few minutes that felt like many minutes.

"I know I might not be your type, I am pretty much a hippie. But, I think it's obvious that I really like you…" she said.

She leaned and kissed me. I immediately started kissing her back and pushed her on the bed, holding her down the way Anarchy and I use to do.

"Wait—wait—just, slow down a little. I mean, I like what you're doing but I'm in no hurry," she cooed.

I'd never been told to slow down before. I loosened my grip on her wrists and she held my hands as we, very slowly, very gently, made-out. I loved having her underneath me and I missed being with someone who wore skirts because it was so easy to slide my hand up her soft leg. When I got between her legs I discovered she wasn't wearing underwear and I decided I liked hippies. I massaged her clit and she made the best noises—breathy, long, moans that were really getting me hot. When I did slide my hand inside her, fucking her, she took my other hand to her throat and we moved together while she looked in my eyes, another thing I never did. She came all over my pants and kissing her right after this made me want her again. I got up, thinking that was it, when she rolled over and got on top of me, ripped off my sweatshirt and my cum-stained pants, kicked my legs apart, and worked her knee into me. It was right against my pubic bone, hitting it in this way that felt so good. She was biting my neck and if I tried to move she'd nail me down. I had no idea she was so strong. Then she slid her skirt off and still in her Go-Go boots and bra started touching herself as she straddled me on her bed. I bucked under her and then she rolled over on her back.

"I need...some music," she said.

"Okay," I nodded.

"Can you...put a...oooohhhh...a record on?"

I got up fast and went to her shelves. But I had no idea which one to choose. She was still on the bed, moaning and getting off.

"Aaaahhhh…hurry, Missy…"

"I don't know which one to choose!"

"Just anyone, aahh, ooohhh…just grab one and put it on!" she cried.

I grabbed a record without even looking at the cover, pulled it out, and put it on. When I reached the bed to kiss her the song rang out from the speakers.

"More than a feelin', when I hear that old song they use to play…"

I froze. But Rodney kept touching herself.

"Oh—that's…cool…not the song I…would, oh… have chose…but it is…ah, ah, ah…really epic…"

She was one of those people who could hold a conversation through anything, anywhere.

"You know…they were…aaahhh…really a…oh, oh, oh…a descent band…" she continued.

I laid beside her, holding her throat and kissing her. Then she got on top of me again, still touching herself. She took her other hand and slid it inside me, thrusting very gently. She leaned in.

"Is this okay? Show me how to make it feel good for you."

She kept pushing more of her hand inside me and I was surprised at how easily I received her. She was really fucking me—me! My entire body was shuddering and I kept running out of breath. I could hear my own guttural moans for the first time as I played with her tits under her bra, my eyes rolling back in my head. She started saying all of these incredibly dirty, sexy things to me.

"Yeah, you like me inside you don't you—you like to move against me with my whole hand inside you—that's right—show me how good it feels—"

I gotta say—I didn't see that coming from a hippie like her. Rodney was going harder and faster and I could feel myself cumming once, then twice.

"That's it, keep cumming for me…" she whispered in my ear.

We were both moaning with Boston still singing, *"More than a feeling…I begin dreaming…"* I couldn't stop. I wanted more of her inside me, punching into me. I noticed the Joan Jett poster again, staring right at me, and I started to feel a little weird. It's not that I didn't find Joan Jett sexy, I just didn't feel that way about her. I always thought if I met her I'd want to look cool in front of her—not like a fucking buffoon trying to keep up with my first real orgasm. Next to the Joan Jett poster was a picture of Patti Smith and next to that was an FBI most wanted poster of Angela Davis and I started to really fucking freak out. They were all watching me and I wasn't sure I could live up to this kind of audience. I shut my eyes really tight and kept moving with Rodney, keying in on the song booming through the speakers.

"Ooooohhhh! I'm gonna cum again! Just keep… grabbing my tits like that…"

And in a matter of seconds, she belted out this incredible, loud, orgasm and ejaculated all over me. Her hand was still moving inside me and out-of-nowhere I felt her deep inside me, so deep I felt like I had to pee. She kissed me and whispered in my ear "Don't fight it baby, just let it happen."

So, I did. I came. I ejaculated for the first time. She lay down next to me and I rolled on top of her and the kissing was the best I'd ever had.

"Are you sure that was your first time being fucked by a girl?" she laughed.

I laughed too but I figured she was just being nice. I was still a suspicious bastard when it came to people being kind to me.

"Dude! She was, like, ambidextrous! She used both hands!" I later told Tommy. I was so excited by my afternoon that I went straight over to Tommy's house after she got off work to tell her the good news.

"I mean—it was fucking crazy. I had no idea what I was doing for half of it but maybe that's what made it feel so good. I'm sorry, is this too much information? I'm sure this happens to you all the time," I carried on.

"Wow, that is crazy," Tommy said, taking a drag off a cigarette on her front porch.

"Fuck dude—I mean, I had no idea she even liked me."

"Yeah, I had no idea Rodney liked you either..." Tommy continued, staring past me.

She kept smoking, then looking down, fidgeting.

"So, did she come onto you or did you come onto her?" Tommy asked in a monotone.

"Well, she came onto me. I mean, we were fucking around with the bass and then we were talking about gold star lesbians, and out-of-nowhere she's like 'you know I like you, right?' and then she starts kissing me and I'm like 'wow...that's...different...'"

I was a clown. One of the many sad clowns immortalized on the side of the freeway back in LA. They juggled fruit. I juggled words, emotions.

"Yeah, yeah I know, I know," Tommy interrupted

Then silence. So much silence.

"So do you wanna go drink or make some food or some shit?" I finally said.

"I gotta go to the bathroom."

Tommy got up quick and went into the house. Sean, Tommy's housemate, came out on the porch.

"You don't get it do you?" Sean said.

"Get what?"

"I heard you—in the kitchen."

"Okay…"

"Tommy has had a crush on Rodney for, like, two years. Like a really bad crush."

I felt really sick.

"She hasn't told her. She's so shy about it. But it's so obvious. I mean, everyone pretty much knows. I don't think Rodney knows, but she should. Are you okay? You don't look so good. I mean, you shouldn't feel bad. You didn't know. You and Tommy have only been friends for like a few months. It's not your fault…" Sean said.

I couldn't hear Sean anymore. All I could understand was the sick churning in my stomach. How I was on my way to fucking up another scene. Fast.

AMORES

I decided to spend less time with Rodney. Tommy was my friend. My only real friend in Santa Cruz. I cared about her. I really wanted to put my best foot forward this time.

I was also hanging out with Christina at school. She said she didn't know the coke she was drinking had alcohol in it, she just thought the soda was flat. I laughed my ass off when she told me that.

"Seriously! I know you think I'm an idiot but, well, I guess I was kind of an idiot. I mean, I didn't ask for no alcohol I just asked if I could have some of what they were having."

Both of us laughed.

"Well, some of my best lessons were learned that way. Hey, by the way, what's up with your roommate?" I said.

"Gabby? She's awesome. I really like her."

"Yeah, but, not to be rude but she seems…"

"Innocent? She is. She grew-up with a single mom who was always working so her abuelita raised her and she was traditional Mexican-Catholic but really nice to her it seems. She left Gabby a bunch of money last year when she died and that's how Gabby can go to school. But yeah, she's definitely innocent. She said she met you."

"Oh yeah?" I was surprised.

"Yeah—she said you were really nice. She obviously doesn't know you!"

More laughter.

"Seriously, well maybe you can invite her to hang out with us sometime. I don't know. She seems like she doesn't have a lot of friends and she's pretty chill."

"I'll definitely do that."

Fate stepped in sooner. Two days after talking with Christina, I ran into Gabby. I was walking back from one of the coffee shops at the college after reading the Chicana Lesbian book Tommy gave me. I'd just decided to end my read that day on Cherríe Moraga's poem "If." I tried to end on a good note whenever I was reading the feminist stuff Tommy gave me because it was usually pretty intense and I didn't know what to do with all the feelings it brought out in me. I had enough to worry about already, I needed to take it easy. Then, there was Gabriella. She was sitting on one of the benches in the sun, the best thing to do on a brisk winter day in Santa Cruz when it actually stopped raining. She was alone, in the field behind the dorms, reading. She had her hair in two braids with a hat on and she was smiling into the book. I couldn't help but watch her for a bit. She was about my height, with curves. She had rich, brown hair, her skin was a beautiful shade of brown. She had dimples. There was a sweetness to her that really took a hold of me. Then she closed the book and as she went to her left to put it in her bag, she saw me. I froze, realizing I was still watching her. She smiled. I smiled back and walked towards her.

"Hi, were you leaving?" I said, a little shy.

"Oh, why, did you want to sit here? Because if you want to sit here it's okay, I can go now. I've been here awhile."

"No, I mean, yes I want to sit here but no I don't want you to leave. I came over to say hi to you," I said.

"Oh, okay," she smiled, surprised.

I sat down. Then it got quiet. I didn't really know what to say, I was never good at breaking the ice. She rescued me from the start.

"Christina said that maybe we should all hang out, that sounds really cool Missy. I don't really hang out very much with anyone except her. My mom says it's because I'm not out-going, I'm kind of a book worm which is a nice way of saying I'm a nerd," she said.

"I like books too. I think it's cool that you like to read," I said.

I sounded like such an awkward idiot. I felt like she was counting on me to hold up the conversation and I don't know, I just felt very drawn to her, like there was another side to her and I wanted to know what that was about.

"You know, your mom kinda sounds like a jerk."

She looked down and was quiet.

"I didn't mean it so harshly," I said ashamed.

"No, no it's not that it's just when you put it like that I guess she does sound that way. It's just she had me when she was really, really young, like fifteen and she and my dad were in a gang and my dad was killed and my mom was left alone with me and she was just sixteen. She just didn't have all the tools, you know? She doesn't mean to be mean. She works a lot to take care of me and if she didn't care about me she wouldn't have left me with my grandmother—she was the best thing for me."

I didn't fully understand all of what she was talking about. Tools? Tools for what? But she sounded sincere and really smart and I liked hearing from her. She was very honest and clear about her feelings. Plus her background, her family—I would never have guessed any of that.

"Yeah my brother is in a gang too. He's locked up right now though," I said.

More silence. I saw the book peeking out of her bag. It was the same Chicana Lesbian book Tommy gave me.

"You're reading *The Girls Our Mothers Warned Us About?*"

Her eyes got big and she smiled again.

"Yes, I saw it at a store downtown and it's just absolutely beautiful, the most romantic poetry. I don't know a lot about Chicana lesbians so when I bought it I thought it was going to be essays, you know, about them, like who are they and what do they do! I'm so stupid sometimes!" she laughed, blushing.

We were both laughing.

"Well at least you had the courage to go into a store and buy the book. My friend practically had to shove this down my throat in order for me to take it. But you're right, it has really beautiful poetry. Like that one by Cherrie Moraga, "If." I really like how it ends, how she talks about being enough. I don't know, I think about that a lot too."

I didn't know why I was telling this girl my secrets. The only person I even came close to talking about my feelings with besides JB was Tommy and right now JB was on tour for months so Tommy was the only one. But there I was, telling Gabby.

"That's so interesting, strange really, because right before you walked up to me I had just finished reading that poem and here you are mentioning it," she said.

That's when she looked right into my eyes and it wasn't long before I decided that I saw her in a very different light.

I'd been hanging out non-stop with Christina and Gabby for the past two weeks and we had made big shroom plans. Gabby had never even smoked a cigarette before so I was a little nervous about her doing them. Christina decided to put her straight-edge life on hold. She had recently started studying the history of psychedelics in one of her classes and she felt the only way to really understand the material was to go all in. This is what happens when you go to a hippie school. Any excuse to go on a mind trip is really an academic exercise or a spiritual retreat.

We were all in the forest, it was afternoon so it wasn't too cold. It had not rained for almost a week so the dampness wasn't there. We dressed warm, brought a blanket, found our privacy, ate the shrooms and waited. Christina felt it first and she was talking about how language looked like colors. Gabby was giggling then laughing a lot and she said every time she laughed little hearts and roses were falling out of her mouth. I was so annoyed because I hadn't felt anything yet. I decided to eat a little more, clearly I had a high tolerance. Christina decided to find a banana slug because the guy who sold her the shrooms told her if she licked one the psychedelic effect would be increased. I stayed on the blanket, waiting for the effect to kick in. Gabby was spinning. Literally standing up and spinning her body around. She looked like an incredible Chicana fairy. I could see her wings. I leaned back and kept watching her morph into a rose, then become mud that sank into the cracks of sidewalk, then come up again out of the ground like tall growing vines up a brick wall, then a rose again, then her, just her, with the sharp rays of light bleeding through the trees. Her head tilted back, smiling, spinning. Then she looked right at me, stumbled a little towards me, fell back on the blanket and we both laid back laughing. So much laughing. I couldn't hear Christina but I felt like she wasn't far. Then we got up, looked at each other, and I knew this was my moment. I'd been thinking about kissing her for the past few days, but I just hadn't built up the courage yet. I cupped her face, brought her to me, and kissed her. She immediately gave me the tongue and I took this as a sure sign that all signs pointed to yes.

We made out on the blanket, me on top of her, devouring her. I wanted to bury my face into all the edges of her neck, her ears, fall into her eyes her mouth her breath—I couldn't stop kissing her. The way she put her hands on me, touched my face—I wasn't gonna hide it anymore. I wanted her.

Just as I was about to take it a step further, I heard Christina howling then run up to us and tell us how she just spent the last hour talking to a highly advanced group of ants who told her that the secret to life is dirt, in particular ant hills. We all started laughing, lay back on the blanket, and watched the shadows of afternoon around us.

I was impressed. The shrooms lasted hours upon hours. It was getting dark and cold and Christina's girlfriend from the Valley down south was on her way to visit and she had to get ready to meet up with her later. When we got back to the dorm, Christina walked ahead down the hall and I grabbed Gabby into me one more time and kissed her told her to come back to my room in an hour. When she returned, I wasted no time getting into bed with her. She also didn't waste any time. She quickly shut my door behind her, locked it, and started taking her clothes off. Having her in bed with me made me realize how alone I'd been. Her body was so soft and warm, she had a round belly and firm tits with dark nipples that I held in my mouth for a long time. She was quiet at first which only turned me on more, but when she whispered in my ear "Will you go inside me?" I almost lost all control. I took it gently, then gained momentum. She was beneath me and I kept watching her face the entire time, the light from a new half-moon shining on her face through my window in the dark. I could feel the moment of pressure inside her against my middle finger and that's when she cried out, hot liquid all over me, my bed, underneath her. Me next to her, wrapped around each other, kissing for hours. I kept thinking about the Cherrie Moraga poem and all the ways I felt myself open right then with Gabby. It wasn't the kinkiest or craziest sex I'd ever had but it was one of the most intimate and I found myself practically high off her and she let me have all of her. She never stopped me, she truly gave herself to me.

In the morning, I felt Gabby still wrapped around me. *Quierda*. Carlos always said that to me. It was the only word I could think of when I thought of her. For a second, I was worried that maybe she didn't like my body because she didn't go inside me or touch me there. But luckily those thoughts were erased when she woke up, slid down between my legs, went down on me first thing in the morning, giving me one of the best multiple orgasms of my life. She wasn't Gabby from down the hall anymore. I had a lover.

I spent the next few weeks immersed in Gabby. Having a lover, a consistent sexual partner, gave me the chance to have a lot of sex. And a lot of sex was had. It was in my room, her room, the back seat of her car at the beach, the field behind the dorm, in the shower together. It was more than sex, it was her. I missed her when I was away from her. I started hating going to the city, having to go to work, because I would much rather be with Gabby, listening to another one of her stories from back in the day, or a new book she was involved with. I definitely cared a lot about her, but I was still keeping secrets. She still had no idea what I did for work in the city and I felt that telling her would ruin everything and I was thinking about quitting for awhile anyway, or taking a break at least. What was the point in telling her, possibly upsetting her, if I was gonna just stop soon anyway? Tommy and the others at

Our Space hadn't met her yet. I wasn't sure I was ready for my worlds to collide. Not yet. It was hard enough dealing with Christina. Gabby had told her we were hooking up and while Christina wasn't against it she didn't seem too excited about it either. She spent less and less time with the two of us and while I wished she would hang out more, I honestly didn't mind having Gabby all to myself. I was totally hung up on Gabriella Santos.

I had decided on my way to work that night that maybe I would take the summer off from the club. I didn't really need money over the summer except to find a place to live for three months. And if worst came to worst and I couldn't find a place in Santa Cruz I would just keep my room at JB's and try writing some of my own poems. I had been reading so many of the books Tommy gave me. I always wrote essays, but I loved the poetry of Xicanisma. I appreciated the mastery of language, the depth—I was starting to see why Tommy called herself a Xicana Feminist. There was a real sense that these mujeres knew all about us. It made me feel less alone.

Not to mention there was Gabby. She mentioned staying in Santa Cruz over the summer too. I figured if we were still hooking up by then, I would ask her to be my girlfriend. I'd never been the one to ask before, so it was on my mind a lot. She was on my mind a lot.

I was at work on another Saturday night. It was slow. Right before taxes were due was always slow. I had just finished taking a break, talking to Gabby on the pay phone at work. I was walking back towards the front of the club when a middle-aged man came stumbling towards me. I figured he was lost so I said, "Hey there handsome, the party is this way, back here is employees only."

He just stared at me, didn't speak. I repeated myself.

"Unfortunately you can't come back here, it's employees only."

He looked me up and down, turned around and headed towards the front. I waited a minute so that he was further ahead of me, then I walked down the hallway back out to the front to do my last round of private dances before heading back to JB's. I wandered around, smiling at the handful of men in the club. Then I saw the man from earlier. I decided to walk by him and not verbally offer a dance.

"Hey, I want a dance," he said as I passed by him.

I turned around and he had his dick out in his hand.

I immediately got angry.

"What the fuck is your fucking problem?"

That's when Ronnie, one of the bouncers, came over and saw the situation. He picked the guy clean up and threw him into the street. There were a few regulars there that night who asked if I was okay. If anything I was more angry. Usually if something like that happened I would just say 'no thanks' and walk away. But ever since I started reading the books Tommy gave me, I allowed myself to feel angry. I was tired of people taking my space, crossing my lines. I had lines, despite the fact that I wasn't perfect. There were lovely ladies who would provide services to you where your dick can be in your hand for a nominal fee and you don't have to waste my time or jeopardize my being at this club because you wanna pull that shit around here.

After about an hour the owner said I could call it a night and he apologized to me for that asshole and I wasn't in trouble for yelling and cussing, which helped a little. I changed back into my street clothes, stashed my cash, strapped my bag across my chest, and I was out into another San Francisco night to hail a cab on Market street. I was on my usual walk, thinking about Gabby, how I could just wake-up in a few hours and catch the bus back to Santa Cruz, maybe take her to breakfast or something nice. I crossed the same alley, past the dumpsters, under the fence, back onto the street and that's when he grabbed me. It was the guy from the club, the asshole who got kicked out. I looked down and he had his dick out again and his hand to my throat.

"You owe me a dance, bitch," he said, and then he pressed his mouth onto mine.

He was trying to take off my pants, it all happened so quickly. But he wasn't much taller than me, and as I looked down at his stuff hanging out I just shut my eyes and kneed him in the groin as hard as I could. He released his grip on me and I fell a little. I got up, but he came after me again. I turned around and hit him with a palm strike as hard as I could—yes, a palm strike, because only at a hippie school can you take Women's Self Defense and use it as an elective credit. It must have worked because all I knew was that he fell back, yelled, and blood started pouring out of his face. I immediately took off running as fast as I could. I kept thinking about things that were fast: lightning again, wind, wind, this time let me be wind, just push me home, just get me there. I kept thinking I could hear his footsteps behind me and I kept running faster. Finally I made it to Market street and a couple was getting out of a cab and I immediately jumped in.

"Seriously, I'm being chased!" I said.

The elderly driver got out, looked down the street, and got back into the cab.

"Honey, there's no one there. Oh my god, child, what happened to you…"

I looked down at myself. I was dirty, my pants were undone, and my right hand, which I used to hit that guy, had a huge gash in the palm, bleeding everywhere. I was shaking.

"Just please take me home."

"I really think you should go to a hospital, dear—"

"I'm not going to a fucking hospital! Just take me the fuck home! Please!" I screamed.

He drove me home with the meter off, and waited for me to get inside my door. There was no point in reporting it. In a way, I felt like I deserved it because what the fuck was I doing with my life anyway? Why did bad shit always keep happening to me, right when the story was getting good? I collapsed in the bathroom at JB's and cried into the shower.

SLEEPING WITH THE LIGHT ON

The hardest part was forgetting. It had been two weeks. I'd gone back to the club to work three times, but each time I was literally looking over my shoulder every five minutes. I could swear I was hearing foot steps behind me. I couldn't get that fucking loser's voice out of my head, 'You still owe me a dance, bitch.'

I also got tested. The gash in my hand was pretty serious, I must have hit bone or something. Everything came back saying I was okay, or at least STD-free. I thought I would feel safe in Santa Cruz but the truth was, I just got more anxious. I kept thinking maybe he followed me to Santa Cruz and knew I was a college girl, where I stayed, maybe he even knew that Tommy was my best friend and wanted to fuck with her too. And Gabriella. All of this fear seemed irrational, my conscious mind knew that the odds of this guy following me down to Santa Cruz were incredibly slim. But my subconscious knew that the odds weren't impossible. I finally told Tommy on her lunch break from Our Space.

"What the fuck—I'm so glad you're okay, but you should've told me sooner, right away," she said hugging me.

"I just…I don't know. I know that people are gonna think I deserved it, that I was asking for it because I'm a stripper."

"Well I don't think that way. I don't think that way at all," Tommy said.

It felt good to tell her. Again, I thought it would make me feel better. But really, I just felt worse. The whole thing just felt more real and the comfort Tommy gave made me believe that all my feelings were dead on. She wanted me to keep talking about it, go see someone who could help. I just couldn't do that. I decided I would just sleep with the light on, stay up more, plan my route very carefully from the club to the train—*no, fuck that, it's a cab, always a cab from now on, out front, right after work,* ready to take me home, I thought. My routines just made me more nervous.

I was fucking up at school again too. All that happened—I wasn't getting any sleep. I couldn't concentrate. I ended up staying up all night somehow thinking I could avoid my fear of the dark only to sleep all day, arrive late to classes or miss them altogether. This time the Dean of Admissions made it crystal clear: figure my shit out by Spring quarter or get the fuck out. I didn't have a home to go to anymore—sure, I had JB's. But the city was becoming my enemy and if I didn't get right quick, I faced more than getting kicked out of school. I finally made friends in the beach town, got to kinda like it even. I went back to drinking, just at night so I could get to sleep. At first, I promised myself it was a temporary solution, a means to an end. It was just for now, just until I finished the last week of finals and after Spring Break.

I hadn't talked to Gabby since it happened. She called. She called everyday. She even left notes on my door at the dorm. I just called her back once, left a message on her machine saying I was too busy and needed to get school shit done. I couldn't face her. I couldn't even tell her, she didn't know what exactly I did for money in the city. I'd have to come out as a stripper and tell her about the attempted assault. She was sort of innocent, I felt bad getting involved with her now because I knew we were just too different. She was sweet, really sweet. Thoughtful. Caring. So nice. I was the opposite of those. I was sour, bitter, insecure, hard, and now afraid. Plus I had real problems to deal with, real grown-ass problems and I would just drag Gabby down with me. I decided to hide a little longer, just until after finals and Spring Break.

I barely passed my classes, but I passed. That was all that mattered and it got the Dean off my back for the time being. Spring Break I spent hiding out in the dorm at school. I was more and more not considering the city as a second home. JB was gone now and the truth was he was right: I was young, real young. I didn't really know how to be on my own even though I always was. I was guessing a lot at how to do the grown-up thing and the loneliness I felt up north versus LA seemed overwhelming at times. Tommy worked a lot, plus still did the band and school. I was seeing less and less of her too. The college was so quiet during the break, it was actually a relief to just walk amongst the trees and not feel like I might run into Christina or Gabby, have them confront me about where I'd been and what was going on. It felt good to be in the Redwoods. The forest I spent so much time being afraid of when I first got there was starting to grow on me. The trees felt like a refuge, I felt held by them.

As soon as Spring quarter started, I felt the anxiety all over again. And I started drinking. A lot. I was drinking all the time, like back when I ran with Anarchy. It was so easy to do too. Half the time nobody even noticed I was drinking in class right out of a coffee cup. The phone calls from Gabby started coming again too and I knew I couldn't out-run her forever.

"Oh my goodness I can't believe I finally caught you. I've missed you. I've been so worried. Did you pass last quarter? Is everything okay?" she said when I finally answered one of her phone calls.

"Yeah, yeah I passed. It's okay for now," I said weakly.

There was some silence. I didn't know what to say. She sounded so excited to hear from me and when she said she missed me, she said it in that soft way that she does whenever she says something really sincere. My heart was warm for a second, but I had already decided it could never work between us. I was too much of a fuck up. I had nothing to offer a girl like her. I was too damaged. Broken. I was nineteen and already felt used up. The poetry I felt for Gabby—I let it go.

"Well, I know the quarter just started and all but I'd really like to see you," she said, always sweetly.

"Yeah, okay."

"When?"

"What?" I said.

"When," she repeated.

"How about tomorrow, I'll meet you downtown at the Nick. We'll see a movie together. Okay? Let's just meet at eight."

"That sounds really nice. See you soon, I love you," she said.

"Yeah, see you soon."

I hung up. I was an asshole. It was the best I could do. Better than saying it and not believing in it. But still a dick move. That night I couldn't sleep. I wanted to drink but I had nothing and the buses stopped running from the school to downtown or anywhere near a liquor store, especially the one that sold to me illegally. I just kept thinking about that fucking guy again, his hands squeezing my arms, grabbing me, pushing me against the wall, hands at my throat, always at my throat, pressing his filthy mouth to me. It was all too familiar. All too much like my childhood when the neighbor in our apartment building use to touch me. I knew it was wrong then too. But I was still convinced that no one would believe me. So I didn't say anything. Eventually he stopped because I got too old and I've been trying to grow-up ever since.

In the morning, all I could think about was the night before. No sleep, all bad thoughts. And a drink was all I could think about for the past eight hours. But the liquor store wasn't open until noon and I had class all day. I went to my classes, shaky. I tried to take notes on everything just so my hands would have something to do and people around me wouldn't notice my shakes so much. The day seemed to drag on forever until finally it was 6pm and I hopped on the bus, went to the liquor store off Laurel that sold to me without an ID, bought my shit, lots of it this time, and cigarettes—I wanted to be in for the night. Just me and my liquid peace. No one to see me, no one to face.

I started drinking on the bus ride home out of a paper bag in the back of the bus. By the time I reached my door in the dorm, I'd already finished half a fifth of vodka and chased it with one of the beers. I was buzzed, but not drunk enough to not feel. So I kept drinking to the door of my building, up the stairs, then to my door. I drank in my room, with my records playing loud on the record player. I just kept slamming it into me. Faster, harder. More more forget forget. An hour later I'd finished everything I bought except for a couple beers. I looked out the window of my room, leaning against the wall to hold me up. My phone was ringing but I never answered it. I turned the volume off the machine. No one to interrupt my self-destruction right now. The phone kept ringing, and I kept looking and leaning and the record player finally stopped playing because that side of the record was over, I was too drunk to flip it over, and I slowly felt my body falling to the floor, my head hitting the thin carpet, my eyes staring at the ceiling with twinkle lights getting blurry in front of me.

I woke up on the floor of my room with a knocking at my door. The knocking was persistent, just wouldn't fucking stop. So I managed to get up and answer it. It was Gabby.

"Oh my goodness are you okay? It's two in the afternoon," she said, worried.

She immediately started to hug me. I just stood there. She brushed her hand across my face and said what I feared.

"What happened to you?"

The question kept repeating in my head, almost like an echo, a ringing. *What happened to you? What happened to you?* She let herself into my room and shut the door.

"I waited three hours for you last night at the Nick..." she began.

Fuck, I thought. *That was last night. Why the fuck did I get myself involved in plans with her? Why did she have to be so fucking nice? The kind of nice that just makes a person like me feel guilty all the time and I'll commit to things I can't keep, just making things worse, and still she won't leave me alone. She kept trying.* That just made me more upset.

"Look, I know that you have a lot on your plate—"

"You're right, I do," I said defensively.

"Okay, well I just—I mean, didn't you get any of my messages? Why would you stand me up like that?" she then leaned into me, putting her arms around my waist. She was trying to kiss me but I couldn't even look at her. I couldn't handle it anymore. She was pushing too much, caring too much. I felt my body tighten and I was having trouble breathing. The more she touched me, the closer she got, the more I wanted to just push her away and jump out the window. I felt cornered.

"I mean, I was worried about you—"

"Okay, I fucking get it. Look, I heard you the first time. You just want to make me feel guilty for standing you up," I said, my voice raised as I took her hands from my waist and backed away from her.

"Is that really what you did?" she sounded hurt.

"I…" I could feel myself wanting to throw-up. I kept looking at her, the look on her face—I couldn't take it anymore. I snapped.

"Look you need to just go, okay! You need to get out of here!" I was shouting now. She kept staring at me, her face twisted as if she was about to cry.

"Fuck, seriously?! Now you're going to cry? What the fuck Gabriella?! Seriously—what the fuck is wrong with you? We hung-out for awhile and some things happened between us but that doesn't mean we belong to each other. You're not my property and you don't fucking own me!" I yelled.

She looked around the room. There were bottles and beer cans everywhere.

"You stood me up so you could get drunk?" she said, weepy.

"No—fuck, just fucking stop okay! Just stop this shit! Gabriella we are not girlfriends! We're not together! There isn't a chance in hell I could ever be with you, with someone whose never even seen a dirty movie before or smoked a joint! Who the fuck do you think I am? Who the fuck do you think you are? I mean, your only friend is your roommate so that should tell you right there how things are going for you. You need to grow-up!"

She started to cry, right there in front of me. I kept going.

"You just don't get it—you're like a child. A naïve child who still acts like they're in high school! You actually think that in this world the two of us would make it together?! I'd have to carry you the whole way, you're always so fucking awkward! And you're so fucking needy! It's a miracle you've made it this far!"

My whole body was shaking. My face was hot. I could feel all the anger pour out of me and onto this girl. She just stood there in front of me, crying. She wouldn't move. So I just grabbed my coat and keys and left her there, slamming the door.

I went downtown to look for Tommy. I went by her house but she wasn't there. Then I went to Our Space but Sheila said she wasn't working today. I kept walking all over downtown, back over to the park and then back to the Metro. I lost track of time and the day. Hours passed and I was still hung-over. I went to the liquor store on Laurel, got my usual fix, and headed back to the college. I got to my door and saw some women from the women's hall where Gabby and Christina lived standing around talking. They all sounded hushed and upset. I couldn't hear what they were saying at first. I was trying just to pass them quickly and get to my room so I could continue to drink.

"They took Gabby to the hospital just now," I heard one of the girls say.

"What? Gabby from down the hall?" I said to the girl.

"Yeah, Christina's roommate. They said she was found on the floor and it looks like she took a bunch of pills. They rushed her to the ER at Cabrillo."

I immediately threw my bag from the liquor store in my room and headed straight back out to the bus stop.

I was frantic. I had to take another bus once I got to the Metro to the hospital because I couldn't find a cab. The trip felt like it was forever. All I could think about were my last hurtful words to her. I hated myself more than ever.

When I reached the hospital I ran into the waiting room and asked the on-duty nurse for Gabby. But before she could answer me, I saw Christina. I ran up to her but the closer I got the more I saw she didn't look happy to see me.

"What the fuck are you doing here?" she asked in a low tone, her face stone.

"I heard about Gabby—"

"You heard about Gabby? What did you hear Missy?" she said.

She was standing in front of me her fists clenched to her sides.

"I just…" I looked around, searching for the words.

"You know she's in intensive care right now, Missy? She took so many pills they had to pump her stomach twice."

I kept looking at her and she stared right back at me. Only she wasn't looking for an excuse or an explanation.

"Why do you act like such a piece of shit, Missy? What the fuck is your fucking problem that you feel like you have to act like a fucking piece of shit anytime some person tries to give two fucks about you?" she shouted.

The few people in the waiting room and nurses started to stare.

"Look, you don't know—"

She interrupted me again.

"I heard you Missy. I heard you yelling at her today. I was walking past your door and I heard you. And I was the one who found Gabby. There was a note. It's none of your business what it fucking said but there was a note. Your name was in it."

She was shaking a little and the look on her face— I'd never seen a face twisted with anger like that before. I could feel other people's gazes on me as I stood in front of Christina.

"Just get the fuck out. Comprende, Missy? Get. The fuck. Out."

She turned around and walked away from me. I was left standing there, no words. I stepped back out into the parking lot, the darkness of another Santa Cruz evening falling all around me with only one parking-lot light dimly blinking above me.

CRUSHED

The next morning my head was killing me, worse than I ever remembered. I woke-up on the floor again, clutching a t-shirt Gabby left in my room a few weeks ago. I'd been meaning to give it back to her but never got around to it. It felt like all I had of her.

It was Saturday, I was supposed to work. I didn't work Fridays anymore, cuts on hours due to more police drama on Stripper Row. Business was bad, but I was good at saving what money I had for times like these because every working-girl knows the ride isn't always smooth and it doesn't last forever.

I called-in sick for the first time, then told JB on the machine I was staying in Santa Cruz. My watch said 10am and though I knew Christina was mad at me, I had to try and see Gabby again.

I took the two buses to the hospital, went right into the ER and asked for her again. The nurse said she was still in intensive care and unless I was a family member I couldn't see her. I could feel myself sinking into complete failure. I couldn't come all this way and leave with nothing. I could feel tears forming. In a desperate effort I put my hand on the nurse's and said "Please, please can you tell me if she's okay?"

The nurse stopped, looked in my eyes.

"She's the same. No better, but no worse," she said in a low-tone.

She took back her hand, along with a clipboard, and walked away.

The rest of the day I spent alone, in my room, listening to every Smiths' song I owned. My head was still killing me and no matter how much aspirin I took it just wouldn't calm down. I wanted to drink, but the thought of doing it right then just made me feel worse so I decided to wait it out. Then the phone rang. It was Tommy.

"Dude! Everybody in town says you've been looking for me! Are you about to go to work?"

It was already 6pm, another day practically gone.

"No, I called in, I'm here. Hey are you around tonight?"

"You forgot didn't you?" Tommy said.

"Forgot?"

"It's okay dude. I know you usually work on Saturday nights! But tonight my band is playing a show at my house again. And I've made another decision: I'm gonna tell Rodney how I feel about her after we play."

She sounded happy, nervous and happy. Giddy about revealing her secret crush to her secret crush.

"But what about Gretch? Hanging-out? And your band, dating someone in your band?"

"Gretch and I were always friends, no strings you know? She's happy for me. Not sure about the band but I don't think it'll be weird. And hanging-out? We'll always hang out! Having a girlfriend isn't gonna change that for me!"

I kept looking out the window for some kind of answer. Tommy kept going on the phone.

"Look, why don't you come tonight and tell me all about what's going on? I mean, you're not working anyway and it's Saturday—just come to Chestnut Street dude. 11pm. We go on at 11pm and play four songs so don't be late! I can't wait to see you, I gotta put my smoke out and head back into the bookstore!"

She hung-up, most likely from the pay phone around the corner from Our Space. I hadn't agreed to come, but I hadn't said I wouldn't either. I lay down again, getting ready for the night.

I showed up to Tommy's about two steps from being drunk. I couldn't show up sober, not tonight. Tommy's new spot on Chestnut was smaller and I knew it would be wall to wall people not just from the college but from Our Space, the punk scene—when I walked up I was right, basically all of Santa Cruz seemed to be at Tommy's house.

"Hey dude!" Tommy said as I made it through the front, then towards the kitchen.

"Hey," I said, half-smiling, smelling like vodka.

"Whoa dude, you already got started I guess!" she laughed as her kitchen counter buffered my wavering.

"You know me," I said.

I held up my hands like I was presenting an award or getting ready to make another big mistake.

There were people everywhere, all the chicks from the feminist bookstore were there and gave me hugs but I just couldn't quite get in the mood. I saw Rodney in the corner, tuning her bass. She was wearing this tight, red dress that fell to her knees, black fishnets with the line going up the back of the leg. Heels. Her long blonde hair slicked back into a smooth ponytail.

"She looks amazing doesn't she? Tonight I'm gonna make shit happen," Tommy said in my ear.

Tommy walked away. I kept staring and then Rodney looked up and caught my gaze. She smiled back, really big. She waved. I turned around to see who she was waving at, but no one was there. Then she motioned for me to come over. The vodka was definitely hitting me, and all the aspirin swimming in my stomach from the last twenty-four hours made me feel even more like I was floating. Rodney hugged me, really tight and close. She smelled liked apples, always apples.

"I've missed you. Where have you been?"

"I've been around," I said.

"Well, don't go anywhere after our set—I wanna talk to you."

"I don't know, I'm pretty drunk, I don't think I'd be much fun," I smiled drunkenly.

"I'm pretty buzzed too, but still gotta play. Really, stick around?"

"I think Tommy wants to talk to you—"

But before I could finish my sentence Rodney was off looking for a cord and setting up amps. I retreated to the front of the house and back onto the porch. The band was getting ready, Tommy was dressed up. Well, for us it was dressed up: the cleanest pair of Dickie's, combat boots, a white button-up shirt with a skinny black tie and a Pachuco-style hat. From far away they looked like a good couple. I started looking around me. There were girls everywhere together. To my right, I could've sworn I saw Gabby. The girl looked so much like her, those soft brown eyes, long brown hair, coco-skin. But I knew it wasn't her. Gabby was in a hospital bed right now, trying to stay alive.

As soon as the band's set was over I pushed myself into one of the bedrooms. I realized I was in Tommy's room and that made me feel safe for a bit. I sat on her bed, retying my laces on my vans since the buses stopped running and getting a cab in Santa Cruz on a busy Saturday night didn't look like an option. I knew I was in for a long walk home. I slammed the last small bottle of vodka I had in my jacket pocket and that's when I really did myself in. That last drink sent me over. I tried to get up, but just couldn't. I lay back on the bed, closed my eyes and tried to let my head stop spinning. I felt a hand touch my face. It was warm, soft. For a moment I thought it was Gabby and we were in the field somewhere. But when I opened my eyes, it was Rodney. I slowly got up.

"Hey. I was getting…comfortable…I guess" I slurred.

My words were coming out so slow, every syllable was work. Rodney kept touching me gently. Her tits half in her dress, half out for all to see. She leaned in and kissed me.

"Wait, I thought…Tommy…" I started.

She kissed me again.

"Now, I'm drunk. Please come over here." She laughed a little.

She laid back on the bed. She looked incredible. Her tight red dress hiked up to her hips, exposing the garters she was wearing. She reminded me of my first crush, Cheri Currie, in the pink lace thing.

"If you don't feel well, I totally understand," she said, giving me what I now know to be bedroom eyes.

"No, no I'm not sick."

I leaned in on-top of her and kept kissing her. She felt so good under me and the only time a girl felt that good under me was Gabriella. I closed my eyes and kept kissing Rodney but all I could see in my mind was mi Gabriella, mi hermosa, her curves, the outline of her thighs. I laced my fingers into her hair, gently pulled her head back and started biting her neck. She released a small moan.

"Oh Missy, yes, this is what I want…"

I kept going and I felt her take my hand and put it up her skirt.

"You know what to do now," she whispered.

I put my fingers in her mouth first and then went inside her, fucking her, even better than the last time. She wrapped her legs around me, I could feel her heel digging into my back. She kept bucking beneath me, going and going and Gabriella kept swirling through my head, la sonrisa de mi Gabby, el pelo y ojos de mi Gabby—all I could see behind my closed eyes was her. Then a loud moan, almost a scream.

"Oh yes Missy, fuck! Oh fuck that feels so good!"

Then she came, all over my hand, my eyes still shut. Light suddenly poured into the room. I turned my head, opened my eyes and it was Tommy in the open-doorway of her room. She just stood there, staring down at me. I turned my head back in front of me, looked down, and it was Rodney beneath me, she had been there the whole time. Gabby was a dream. I turned to look back at Tommy but before I could say anything she said "I'm really happy for you," and then took off.

Rodney was still beneath me, my hand still half-inside her.

"Fuck. Look, I gotta go Rodney," I muttered.

I wiped my hand off on my shirt and once again stumbled out of a house that wasn't mine, leaving a mess of swirling ashes from the bridges I'd burned right behind me.

LLARONAS

There was a really sick feeling in the corner of my stomach that I've had since forever. I could feel it when I realized Gabby was gone from me and this time it was because of me. I heard through some of the girls down the hall that she was gonna be okay but had to leave school. I officially fucked up. I would say I officially drove someone crazy but that would be mean and dismissive. And a lie.

I sat in the large meadow behind one of the dorms. Looked out into the horizon beyond all the vastness of green grass and trees. Always the trees, towering and holding all my secrets. I never thought I would come to like nature, the forest. The only things that managed to hold me anymore were those trees and the sky in all its colors. I kept staring, thinking how on April twentieth this meadow is filled with happy pot-smokers. But now it's empty. Just me and a lot of thoughts, guilt, and regrets to fill it. And while it's overwhelming, it's not enough to let you escape.

I couldn't escape Gabriella. Everything reminded me of her and I didn't fucking know why. I thought maybe I loved her. But I'd loved before. At least once. Gabriella didn't feel like that. But when I was with her, I liked it. I liked who I was. When I went to bed with her, that was making-love. I would get lost in her beneath me and I was always careful when touching her because I had learned enough by now that there are parts of a woman that, when touched a certain way, either made her fall apart or set her free. I wanted to be free with her.

But I couldn't. I had scars too. I had an ego and a dirty mouth. I didn't know how to be loved. I didn't even have friends, let alone a best friend, until six or seven months ago and I couldn't even get that right. Once again I was alone and it was all my fault.

I couldn't stop thinking about Tommy either. Or Christina. But, that day at the hospital made it clear that I had no chance of anything with Tina. I went to the café on campus and saw Christina. She saw me too. Looked right at me. That look on her face—it wasn't that she hated me. It was just a look I had seen too many times by now. The same look Tommy gave me at the party. The look Carlos gave me right before he left my apartment, left me. The same look I would've given Anarchy but she probably saw that coming and took off before she could see it, see me, and be haunted forever. Now Christina. After I saw "the look" I just turned around and left. I haven't seen her since, even though she's down the hall. I don't have to avoid her. I know I don't exist anymore and that's fine.

Meanwhile, I was in deep with all my other shit. The club was cutting hours left and right due to crackdowns by the city of known "vice areas." Stripper Row in SF looked emptier every week. I was working only one night, just a few hundred dollars. I was making enough to get by and maybe that was okay. I didn't need more money because I had no friends. Instead it gave me more time on my hands, which made my loneliness almost unbearable.

There were only six weeks of school left. For the whole year. Then summer. It was hard enough dealing with the city three days a week. I couldn't imagine it day-in, day-out for three long months. JB would be gone. Touring, like always. But, it would be a good place to hide. And I'm good at being small.

Then shit really hit the fan.

I was on my way to class, rushing. I dropped a book. A note fell out. It was from Gabby. She always did stuff like that. She'd write a really sweet note and hide it somewhere. Under my typewriter in my room. In my sock drawer. A book. She'd never tell me. Sometimes it took weeks for me to find one and she never said a word, never let on, never asked about it. I'd find them, these treasures, when I least expected it. And I'd found another one.

"You are the most amazing brilliance I've ever seen. I'm so happy I met you."

Dated two weeks before she took all those pills in my honor.

I couldn't stop staring at the yellow notebook paper, the words written in her delicate hand-writing. It was then I really cried. I got on the ground, crumbling

135

the letter in my hand, my head buried into my arms, sobbing. I didn't even look to see if I was alone. I didn't care anymore. I was getting so sick of being invisible. I was in the forest, my only friend now. I decided the trees could have my tears. They lived near salt-water. They could handle it. They were old too. They'd seen a lot of heartbreak, I was sure I wasn't the first. They could handle that too.

I cried, right there in the dirt, the sky fading into nighttime. The soft white safety lights coming to life around me, but I was still in the dark, still hidden, kept. It was cool, crisp, which felt good on my face. I thought about my mother and father, how I hadn't spoken to them since I left last year. Me coming out to them in their living room after high school graduation. My father telling me it was okay, but my mother telling me it wasn't. My father in the middle, making secret phone calls to me from pay phones to see how I was doing so my mother wouldn't know. My mother never saying a word. Me never saying a word. Espi and all her kids. One brother in jail today, maybe prison tomorrow. The other brother I had no idea. NaTanya long gone before we ever really began. My first love. Skins and their racism, this town, the ocean so loud, this school and its privileges, all the punk scenes, the city, don't get me started on the fucking city. Anarchy, Carlos, ache, ache, JB always gone, alone, drinking too much, losing friends, losing faith, being an asshole, hurting Tommy, disappointing, hurting Gabby, hurting Gabby, fucking over Gabby—it's no wonder I decided to go on one.

I picked myself up off the ground and put the note away. I went to the bus stop instead of class. Went downtown to the Metro. Got someone to buy me booze this time, a lot of it, scored a few pills. Went to the park and got very drunk. Somehow I managed to walk to a punk house on the other side of the park I heard would have a house-show. And as I entered the house, not even ten feet away from me was Carlos.

I couldn't fucking believe it—what the fuck was he even doing in Santa Cruz? In my mind I wanted to quickly duck into a hallway or out the front. But I was already really drunk. The walk hadn't quite sobered me up like I'd hoped. Now I was in this house, with Carlos right there and I didn't have the reflexes or instinct to move fast enough. I just leaned against a wall and hoped he wouldn't see me. I saw a really young punk girl, a Chicana, sidle up to him. I recognized the girl from shows and I saw her a couple times at the college, I think she went there too. She stood in front of him, his arms wrapped around her, smiling, kissing her neck sweetly while they watched the band. I saw the word "Carlos" tattooed on her neck. I didn't realize I was actually staring at them until Carlos looked up from her and saw me. I wasn't sure if he was looking at me but I couldn't stop looking at him. He stared back at me with those eyes of his that I remember falling into. Again, my mind told me to get the fuck out of there but my body just couldn't get the job done. I kept staring and he quickly looked away, then looked at me again. Then the girl, his girl, turned around and suddenly kissed him. He kissed her back. They looked right into each other and he was smiling.

I decided I'd had enough. Before I could see if Carlos was looking back or even coming my way, I managed to make it out the front door, onto the side walk and headed back to the park. I didn't cry. But I felt low. So low. And a little jealous. More because I just couldn't seem to have anything simple or lovely. At the park, I did the pills. I sat under the tree Anarchy used to always find me under and I waited. Waited to feel nothing. I felt very dizzy and I fell back onto the ground, the tree branches waving, the sky swirling above me. I started having trouble seeing. Then I saw a shadow above me. For a second I thought it might be a ghost, just what I need at this point. I felt tugging on my arms, like I was being pulled up. I kept resisting. The tugging got a little harder, then some murmuring, like a voice, only I couldn't make out the words. More tugging and this time, I could feel more hands on me and I panicked, started kicking, swinging my arms. But I didn't have much strength right then, and then one of the shadows said, in a blurry whisper "Relax, relax, it's me…just me…it's alright…"

I woke up to a Tribe 8 poster in front of me on the back of a door. The sun was bleeding onto my legs and I could feel a light breeze above me. I was in bed, only it wasn't my bed. I rubbed my eyes, found my glasses next to me, and started investigating where I'd landed this time. Then the door opened. It was Tommy.

"Hey, I need you to take this," she said, holding a glass of water and aspirin in one hand and what looked like orange juice in the other.

She persisted.

"Seriously, I need you to take this."

I rolled over, my back to her. She put the glass down.

"Please, stop fighting. Just take this stuff," she said gently.

I rolled back over, slowly got up. Swallowed the pills, downed the water, then took the orange juice and began drinking it. Only it wasn't orange juice and after one sip I quickly got up, ran to the bathroom and vomited. A lot.

"Works every time. It's the best hang-over cure I ever created! I'm late for work!" I heard Gretch yell from the front porch before she took off on her bike.

I cleaned up and went back into Tommy's room. It just occurred to me that, like always, I had no pants on.

"You can wear these," Tommy said, handing me a pair of her faded blue Dickie's.

"Do I even want to ask what happened to my pants?" I groaned.

"I'm washing them. You threw-up on those last night too," she replied.

I put the Dickie's on, sat down, found my jean jacket on the floor and fished in the pocket for a cigarette.

"Thank you," I managed to push out, looking at the floor.

"Sure. How do you feel? Gretch said it's a full-proof hangover cure. You just take what you need to get it out of you. Do you need more?" Tommy asked.

"No. No, one sip was definitely enough. But I think I might have puked up those aspirin I just took." Tommy laughed a little.

"Yeah, I didn't think about that. Let me get you a couple more."

She left her room again and I found the smokes, got up, slowly, very slowly, and shuffled to the front porch. She met me out front.

"Here you go." She handed them to me.

I took them again. Then Tommy lit a cigarette and we just sat on her front porch on Chestnut Street, the traffic on Laurel softly passing by in the distance. There was a lot of silence, and if it wasn't for my cigarette I would've guessed I'd been sitting there for hours instead of ten minutes. I knew I had to break the ice. I knew it was my responsibility, but I was having trouble being brave. For a moment, I actually considered doing something really rude just to get her to kick me out of her life for good so I could be free from having to face her. I was a fucking punk-ass. But Tommy being the amazing chingona she was decided to let me off the hook.

"Look, I don't care about Rodney. And I already had one foot out the door with the band anyway."

I kept looking away.

"And maybe I overreacted, Missy. I mean, it's not like Rodney was my girlfriend or anything romantic to me. I didn't have the right to stake a claim on her. She obviously liked you and I mean, who wouldn't? You're funny, talented—"

I interrupted her.

"Don't do that. Don't say all that shit. It's not true," I said. Tears started to form but I was doing everything I could think of not to let them fall.

"You know you shouldn't do that, hide your feelings. You don't have to do that."

I finally found the guts to look at her.

"I'm sorry. I'm really fucking sorry," I said, crying.

And there it was. I'd said it. And meant it. Then the unthinkable happened, at least to me: she hugged me. A real hug. I couldn't stop crying. She held me. I let her. I didn't know this was how any of it would feel.

"It's okay. I forgive you. Forget it," she said.

I sat up and wiped my face clean with my t-shirt. I felt hungry, like I hadn't eaten in days.

"It's kinda late for breakfast stuff, but it's Friday and we could go get pizza or something. I know you usually go to work but you said you only work Saturday nights so maybe you wanna stick around until tomorrow and just hang out? Gretch and some of the others are probably coming over after closing the café. We could all just hang out," Tommy said.

It was the best offer I'd heard in a long time.

XICANA CON EQUI

The following month I laid very, very low. I spent most of my time in my room trying to catch up on every school assignment—I thought about what JB said, how I should give it a year and decide. I wanted to stay, at least another year, see what happened. But I couldn't do the club just then. I had enough money stashed away. I figured I could just take the summer off. I told JB two days after he got back from months of touring and after an epic two days of me telling him everything that happened since he'd been gone, even the assault.

"You're sure about this?" he said.

"Yeah, it's just for a few months. You know, maybe get my head put back together a little bit."

"You don't have to leave this place though," he said, a little whiny.

"I'm not leaving. I'm just taking a break," I said, smiling

The club seemed to take the news the same way. They heard about what happened to me and even though it hadn't happened since, they didn't blame me. Plus, I was told I could come back if I wanted to. I thought

I might. Right then I was too angry. Just being in the area of the club made me angry, stressed—I decided it wasn't worth a few hundred dollars.

But money was a continuing reality for my ass. I needed a job over the summer, so I didn't spend all my savings and school money. Just something easy, no big deal. A pay the rent deal. I applied to the first job I saw at the college over the summer, to be on the work crew that cleaned and repainted the dorms on campus for the coming Fall quarter. It sounded easy enough, no experience necessary, and it paid seven dollars and hour. One of the highest paying summer jobs I could find with my clothes on. A week later an older, white hippie dude called me and said I had the job.

"Are you sure you don't want to interview me?"

"No, that's okay. The job is pretty simple, I usually just give it to the first ten people who apply and if that doesn't work out, I got a budget to finish regardless. But don't worry about that. See you in two weeks," he said.

Getting a place to live over the summer turned out to be just as easy. Gretch was gonna be gone a lot over the summer so she asked if I would just be her roommate, pay two-hundred a month, and call it a day. It was gonna be cool because she had a girlfriend in the city and a job at another strip club off Stripper Row closer to downtown, and she would be gone four days a week. I'd basically have my own place. Tommy said she could help me move. I wasn't drinking hard alcohol, only a couple beers at a time, here and there. That was harder, but it kept me out of trouble and if I was going to someday face Gabby, I wanted to be at my best.

Gabriella. I missed her so much. She was always in my thoughts, in every poem I read. And wrote. I realized after talking to JB, Tommy, and Gretch that I was full of shit.

"You fucking love her!" Gretch shouted.

"Is that what's going on?"

Tommy was smiling.

"I think so dude."

"But she left school, I don't even know if she's coming back. Christina hates my guts. I don't think I'll get my chance to tell her."

"I don't know. I mean, Santa Cruz has a lot of intense energy, you know? Things kind of have a way of working themselves out here," Gretch said. Her face scrunched from the sun in her eyes.

I wanted to believe her. For now though, I had school to finish. I had to come up with a project that showed how I'd changed over the past year. Not only did it have to be fucking fabulosa because I spent so much time being a disaster, it also had to have a visual component and be accessible to the community. *I fucking hate you Santa Cruz,* I thought.

I really had no idea how I was going to wrap this hippie shit up. I kept thinking about my new-found mentors, the muxeres in the Chicana Lesbian book Tommy gave me. I kept thinking about interviews I found of Gloria Anzaldúa, la maestra, talking about creating This Bridge Called My Back—how just having a book out there with women of color was radical in itself. I thought about Riot Grrrl, the anger and disappointment I felt trying to be one of them, neither one of us really capable of even beginning a dialogue.

But my love for the music and culture remained, and in order not to feel ashamed about it, I kept trying to figure out how I could do what Cherrie and Gloria did—how I could reclaim it.

"I think I'm gonna do a zine," I told Tommy.

"What?! Dude that's a great idea! You tell the best fucking stories! What's it gonna be about?"

"I'm still figuring that part out, but I was thinking of calling it Xicana Con Equi. But that's probably a stupid title…"

"What the fuck, don't say that! It's your first zine, call it whatever you want. I like the title."

I went to work, really went to work. I wrote the zine about a lot of things. I told the story of Anarchy, I talked about the book Tommy gave me, I talked about my Brown neighborhood and coming out to my parents and not speaking to them all year, I talked about Chicanos in punk rock, I even wrote a short story about the assault. I wasn't brave enough to say it was me. I put a poem, a love poem, about Gabriella in it, though I changed her name too because I didn't have a lot of courage. I talked about Xicana Feminism and how I was going to make it my priority, even though I wasn't sure how I would do that yet. Tommy even got me to sell it in Our Space, and they did a little party for me and I read from it and everything. That was the first time I'd ever done something like that. I got extra credit because Our Space sold it to the community and I pretty much paid Tommy back in thin-crust pizza slices for the next few days for helping me out like that. Tommy was a homie, my homie, my homegirl. I had a homegirl now.

Of course what I realized I really wanted was a girlfriend. That wasn't exactly true. I wanted Gabriella. I pinned a copy of the zine to the bulletin board of Gabby's old room with Christina. I put Gabby's name on it. I walked by the next day and the zine was gone, I only hoped it would make its way to her.

To make things even more interesting, I got a letter from my mom. Almost a year later. It had been sitting on my desk for a few days, unopened. I decided just to go right to the ending. That would tell me if the letter was good news or bad news. I went to the last page and the end said:

I miss you, please take care of you mija, call me anytime. Love, Mami

I sat back on my bed in relief. I put the letter in a box, maybe a paragraph a week, that's how I'll start this with her. Paragraph a week.

My room was in fragments. I was taking down the few posters, throwing my clothes in trash bags. I really didn't own anything and to be honest I liked it that way. It felt good to come out with, at least, what I came with.

Tommy and her Toyota corolla rolled up downstairs. I still had Gabby's shirt. Everyone was trying to move out of the dorms but at this point, half the people were already gone.

I wanted to keep it, but I thought maybe it would be my last desperate attempt to reach Gabby. I'd seen Christina and her girlfriend moving things out, but I couldn't see what car or where they were exactly. I went by their room anyway, saw that no one was in there but that a few items were still waiting to be packed. I quickly ran in the room, put the t-shirt on what used to be Gabby's bed, and then quickly left, back down the hall to my part of the dorm. Tommy was already waiting for me outside my door.

"Is this all you got, dude?" she said in disbelief at my two boxes of books, one crate of records, typewriter, and three trash bags of clothes and blankets.

"Yeah—but could you imagine me trying to haul all this shit on the bus, compa? I mean, seriously!"

We both started laughing. Tommy already had two trash bags and a box in her arms.

"I'll meet you downstairs," I told her.

I went back in my room and looked out the window one last time. My father always said it's good to trust gut instincts, and he was right because that's when I saw her. Gabriella. She was down near the parking circle, wearing jean shorts, her hair in two braids, sandals, and a white lacy shirt. She still looked amazing. I wanted to run down there and speak with her but right behind her were Christina and her girlfriend, putting in the last load of stuff from their room. Gabby had her car packed with all their stuff. I kept staring at her, always staring, but I couldn't move. Then I saw Christina give her the shirt I'd left upstairs. Gabby looked at it, touched it for a second, and then shook her head, threw it in her back seat, and stood smiling at them. They hugged her. Both of them hugged her at once. It was then I knew, I knew the damage I'd done. The three of them got in her car, and drove away.

I sat on the bed the school gave me one last time, and cried. It was all I had in me, probably because I figured I didn't have the right to cry about what happened and that was turning out to be a lesson nobody seemed to be able to teach me. I just had to feel it.

I met Tommy downstairs with the rest of my things. We unloaded at Gretch's and Tommy looked at her watch.

"Dude, it's like really early and I kinda gave you my day because I thought this would take awhile—you wanna go to the beach? There's a bonfire after the Dyke March tonight, we already missed the march."

"Yeah, but maybe we could go hang out the two of us first?"

"Sure," she agreed.

We walked out to the sand on the East Side, found a spot, and sat. Tommy brought a thick, Mexican blanket and wrapped it around us. I imagined it was my cocoon as we sat, staring out at the water, the sun just down.

"I'm never gonna see her again, you know, Gabby, will I?" I mumbled.

"I honestly don't know dude. Maybe, maybe not."

Tommy took another drag off a cigarette. I wiped my eyes, kept looking down, then Tommy put an arm around me.

"C'mon dude, you're way too young for never. Besides it's 1997, and it's the beginning of summer. We got an entire season of book-selling and dorm-painting to enjoy!" she shouted, squeezing me a little.

I looked out at the waves and let the future happen.

Winner of the People Before Profits Poetry Prize, Meliza Bañales is originally from Los Angeles. She was a fixture in the San Francisco spoken-word and slam communities from 1996-2010, where she became the first Xicana to win a poetry slam championship in 2002 and gained national recognition for her appearances on NPR and The Lesbian Podcast. She has toured with Sister Spit: The Next Generation as well as Body Heat: The Femme Porn Tour. The author of *Say It With Your Whole Mouth* (Monkey Press, 2003), she also has work in *Without A Net: The Female Experience of Growing-Up Working Class, Baby, Remember My Name: New Queer Girl Writing, The Encyclopedia of Activism and Social Change,* and *Word Warriors: 35 Women Leaders of the Spoken-Word Movement.* She is a community builder with Con Fuerza, a radical, Xicana Feminist collective in East LA. This is her first novel.

ACKNOWLEDGEMENTS

This book was written in many journals over the course of six years, through two countries, ten states, fifteen cities, through homelessness, poverty, unemployment, minimum-wage jobs, chronic illnesses, handicaps, abuse, four relationships, healing, recovery. All of this happened while writing this one book and I thank every loving ancestor, falling star, and full moon for making sure that despite not having a computer, or a room of my own, I was still able to write this story.

Thank you to Dr. Carol Queen, Simon Shepard, and Lori Selke for the wonderful erotic reading series Perverts Put Out at The Center for Sex and Culture in San Francisco where excerpts of this work were first read and commissioned in 2009. This was where I wrote the first story, "In Regards to Anarchy," which became a chapter in what is now a novel in your hands.

Mil gracias to Rios De La Luz for publishing me on Ladyblog which led to my novel being published. Mil gracias to mis compas: Alma Rosa Rivera (for being the one person besides my editor to read this manuscript and tell me the real deal) and Patty Delgado (for my website and endless problem-solving around this book).

Thank you: 90's Santa Cruz (Jeanette, Kaylah, Ruby, Rae, Genine, Melanie, the beach, the redwoods, Herland, punks, Riot Grrrl, Xican@s dykes and queers), 90's San Francisco (Lynn, Daphne, Tribe 8, Spitboy, North Beach, the Mission, the fog, wet streets, buildings, smoky back rooms, naked ladies, more punks, more dykes and queers, a few Xicanos), Iraya

Robles, Nicky Click, The Lady Ms. Vagina Jenkins, Jen Cross, Alex Cafarelli, Kathleen Delaney-Adams, Ami Mattison, Damien Luxe, Heather Acs, Pamela Peniston, Orson Wagon, Tina D'Elia, Leah Lakshmi Piepzna-Samarashinha, Maya Chinchilla, Esteban Allard-Valdivieso, Pony Lee, Dr. Gloria Anzaldúa, Michele Serros, Elizabeth Stark & Angie Powers (for the awesome podcast on this book), Melinda Adams (for the radio promotion of this book), SOMA Arts, The Center in San Francisco, The Lexington Club (where I wrote an award-winning short film with a compa and a chapter of this book, "Riot Grrrls and Gold Stars" at the bar), Con Fuerza Collective (mi muxeri@), La Concha in East LA, and the LA Femmes of Color Collective (mis femmeanas).

Thank you to my Pop, Mom, and my brothers.

A special thanks to mi hermana, Rosario Le'on. I was able to finish this book because of you, carnala— thank you for almost twenty years of friendship and artistry.

A very special thank you to Ladybox Books and Constance Ann Fitzgerald, one of the best editors and writers I've encountered. I truly appreciate your support of me and this work.

An earlier version of "In Regards to Anarchy" was also a chapbook and performance piece for the East Coast Body Heat Tour, 2010; "In Regards to Anarchy" and "Fossils" were performance pieces at The Berkley Slam, 2010, The Starry Plough, Berkley, CA; Lyrics & Dirges, 2012, Berkeley, CA, Pegasus Bookstore; and The News, 2013, San Francisco, CA, SOMA Arts.

Thank you for reading.